# CHILDHOOD FRIENDS

A NOVEL

BEAUFIELD BERRY

agribella
orbis

Audrey!
I can't tell you
how my heart
smiled to see your name.
Thank you so
much, girlfriend!

Take care of those
mountains for me.
With love,
Beaufield
Berry

04/100

Childhood Friends


This book is a work of fiction. Names, characters, businesses, organizations, places, events, and incidents either are the product of the author's imagination or are used fictitiously. Any resemblance to actual persons, living or dead, events, or locales is entirely coincidental.

For information contact:
**http://www.beaufieldberryfisher.com**
**http://www.agribellaorbis.com**

Book and Cover design by AgriBella Orbis Publishing
ISBN: 978-0-9985962-0-4

First Edition: January 2017

*These pages are dedicated to the 14-year-old girl with the typewriter.*

*"If you want to learn what*
*someone fears losing,*
*Watch what they photograph."*

*Anonymous*

# 1

## Somewhere in Middle America

THE PLANE BOUNCED A LITTLE WHEN THE WHEELS TOUCHED DOWN. It woke me up.

I looked out the window. Speckles of rain, sliding across. Gray day in Omaha.

This was already a mistake. I should've gone somewhere warm, and tropical and foreign.

The light dinged, and everyone on the plane stood up in unison, as though that would get them out of here quicker.

As though any of them wanted to be landing in Omaha.

*We just can't wait to be here!*

I stayed seated. Rooted firmly in to the window seat, I stared into the abyss of a town that raised me and wondered what I'd done to deserve to be back.

I wasn't back. I was just here.

Where had I heard that before?

My mom was picking me up.

My mom, without the cell phone or a proper navigational system or a watch or a working car clock, was picking me up. I expected this to work against me as I bumbled my way to the escalators. I say I bumbled, because on my full flight somehow they'd let me carry on the whole of my luggage. Heavy and complicated and all on my back. Everything I owned that I could get away with, I was carrying. Tripping, swaying back and forth, like Jesus and his cross.

If that wasn't bumbling I didn't know what was.

I pictured myself tumbling down the escalator with all four of my bags, tripping over my shoes or something. I took the elevator. When it opened, the back of my mother was standing there.

"Mom?"

She turned around, startled, and hugged me -- hard and immediate.

"Baby girl!"

She pulled in tighter.

"Hi," she whispered in my ear.

"What are you doing here? On time?"

"Oh, stop," she said defensively. "I'm getting better."

My mother, the sixty-year-old work-in-progress.

"Give me some of those bags."

I handed them over to her without an argument and watched her bumble with them herself.

My mother was adorable. There was no way around that. She had a kind, round face that had always betrayed her age. You knew just what she had looked like as a toddler. The same deep, light eyes, still curious and foolish after decades of living. Her voice was soft, soothing, and nuanced.

Her black hair was barely streaked with gray and usually covered by a scarf, an Aunt Jemima style that she could get away with.

"We'll both take some," I laughed, relieving her of some weight.

"You look beautiful," she kissed my forehead.

"Do I? I feel like shit ran over twice."

"What does that mean? That doesn't make any sense. Who's going back to see what it looks like?"

She wrapped her arm around me and we walked out together into the dismal Midwest October.

"Of course it's raining," I complained.

"It's supposed to be sunny tomorrow; you brought the sun."

"We'll see."

Mom was illegally parked right in front of the doors, where you were only supposed to drop off, pick up and not leave your car. The airport police officer was standing there writing her a ticket.

"Ma'am! You can't park here. This is a drop-off zone."

"It is? I just had to help my daughter. I was in there for five minutes. I've never done this before. I didn't know," she prattled off excuse after excuse in her too-calm voice. A voice that, whether she was playing him or not, sounded truly ignorant of any wrongdoing.

"It's my daughter," she pleaded, as though he must have surely understood the necessity of helping a fully-grown, capable woman with two carry-ons, a backpack, and a large purse.

He stopped, sighed and nodded toward the car.

"This is your warning," he reprimanded, backing away and looking up the row for anyone he could pass the ticket off to.

"Thank you, thank you," she smiled and ushered us both into the Jeep, which was packed with everything from groceries to blankets to random wood.

"Mom, you're too good. You have to know you can't park here."

"The prices they charge to be in the parking garage are ridiculous. Then you have to remember where you parked, then you have to wait in line -- it took us no time. This city doesn't need any more of my money."

"Okay," I said, giggling. My mother, the con artist. "What's all this stuff?" I looked over my shoulder.

"Oh, just my things. Things I need."

"There's a birdcage back there."

"Would you stop being so nosy, please?"

"You're a hoarder."

"It's not hoarding if it's in the car. You can only house hoard."

I accepted her educated opinion on the subject with a scoff and an "Okay."

"How long do you think you'll be here?"

"Tired of me already?"

"Just want to make sure you're not leaving again."

She looked at me with true concern. That worried look your mom gave you that made you feel guilty for nothing. And loved for nothing.

"One-way ticket, Mom. I don't know."

"Is this everything?"

"No. Yes?"

I shook my head, trying to make sense of the confusion I was feeling.

"This isn't everything I have; Alex said he'd order me a POD and have everything moved out here for me when I want."

"What's a POD?"

"It's just a moving company."

"Oh."

"I just don't know if I want anything else."

"All your things?"

"I just brought 300 pounds of useless shit with me. What more do I need?"

"Okay, okay with the s-bombs."

I could tell that was lost on her. The queen of stuff. There always could have been more. I didn't have many things left behind in my house in Austin, anyway. Some Ikea dressers, a bed -- shit like that. Shit my mom had more than enough of. Most things were mutually owned by Alex and me, anyway; he could sell it all, and I wouldn't miss it. I brought my favorite dresses, a million books I'd never read again, journals, and my laptop for work if I was needed. And of course, my camera, my never-leave-home-without-it. When I thought of my big things, they already felt like someone else's.

"I made turkey burgers. I thought we could watch a movie together tonight."

I smiled over at her profile. Her little bumped nose and filled-out lip line. All the times I looked at her from the passenger side of a car while she talked about dinner and movies.

"That sounds perfect. Do you have a movie you want?"

"Something old. I've been taping them."

"You have a DVR?" I asked incredulously.

"Oh no, no, no. I have them taped on VHS. What's DVR?"

I laughed and shook my head. I was longing to lose myself in this sweet, uncertain simplicity.

# 2
## Childhood Bedroom

My mom's house was my childhood home.

It had gone through many transformations, yet somehow was always the same. The paint rotated almost yearly. The knick-knack collection grew and the bedroom's purposes altered, but nothing really ever *changed.*

My bedroom had been a crafting room, a yarn room, a guest room, a music room, and a closet in the fifteen years since I had left. I expected to come home and find it filled with Tupperware or jewelry or whatever Mom's new momentary passion was.

I creaked open the door, one suitcase in hand, and dropped my head in shock. Mouth open. It was the same frothy pink we had painted it years ago, when I was thirteen and said I was in love with that stupid color. No doubt the same can of paint. My old, floral bedspread had returned to the twin-sized wooden daybed; the tube television I proudly purchased was there. All my ridiculous boy-toy posters were back on the wall. Usher, JT, JC, BSB, NKOTB, and, of course, JTT.

"Mom!" I yelled with a laugh in my voice, already hearing her training up the stairs. "What year is it?"

She showed up behind me with a giant smile.

"Do you like it? It's just the way it used to be."

"When I was a kid."

"Yup, that paint is the same paint can," she was too proud.

"That's not a bragging right."

I immediately got flashbacks of my adolescence there. Opening the windows, the cool summer air would come through as I lay on the floor, dreaming of how cool men were and listening to Elliott Smith or Barenaked Ladies. I was weird. I was romantic and sappy and quickly disappointed. I was also boy-crazy and obsessed with the heartthrobs of my generation. All that coming-of-age.

"This is so damn over-the-top, Mom."

"It's fun, huh?"

"Yeah, it's fun."

"I was happy you said you were coming home. Maybe I got carried away. Obviously, I wish it were under other circumstances," her eyes and mouth drooped a little.

"I'm happy to be here, under any circumstances," I rubbed her shoulder.

"You can unpack later. Let's eat."

I happily abandoned the chore and followed her down to the kitchen. The kitchen that had seen a spectrum of colors and was currently settled into an appetite-inducing yellow.

Golden yellow, not 1950s yellow. Natural yellow, not Crayola yellow. Dandelion, not piss.

The cabinets were a forced-antiqued white, and the knobs were turquoise blue.

We sat down to our usual seats at the table. A habit. Including a space for my grandmother's memory. Josephine. Our third, who -- six years after her passing -- was still a powerful presence in the house that we all once shared. She sat at the head. We surveyed the food and eyed each other with famished grins. We could say so much without words. It made our phone conversations taxing.

"So, what do you want to do here?"

"Survive," I laughed. She didn't. "Okay. I just want to relax. Really. I've been working so hard lately, and I need to just chill."

"That's smart. You have to mind your rest."

"I don't even know how to sleep in anymore."

"That doesn't sound like you."

"I'm sure I can pick it up again."

"Yes. Now, what about your friends?"

"Who?"

"Shep and Stassi -- have you talked to them? Are they going to be around?"

"Umm, I don't know. I haven't told them I'm here."

"Why is that? I'm sure they want to see you."

"Because I want to chill, remember? I'll tell them eventually."

"Okay. Well, that's good. What's Shepherd up to?"

"Oh, wow, I have no idea."

"You don't talk to him?"

"I do. I mean, he's not up to anything. The same old."

"You know," she said, slow and thoughtful, "he deserves love." A snort escaped me.

"What?" she asked defensively. "Does he not?"

"No. He does. He does deserve love. I mean, it's a weird thing to say."

"So -- I just have hope he finds the right girl."

"I hope that, too. But also, why are we talking about this?"

"That was never going to be you."

"I know this."

"Does he?"

"Of course he does. That was twelve years ago."

"Well, it just seems like he hasn't had a girlfriend since."

"He's had girlfriends."

"You're a hard act to follow."

"Well, no shit."

"And what's Stassi up to?"

"I don't know that, either. Raising kids, being Stassi, I guess."

"She is just so sweet."

I nodded with that face you made when your mom didn't know a thing you knew, but you wanted to protect her innocence so you held it in.

"She's married, right?"

"You were at the wedding."

"She deserved love."

"What is this? Your new thing?"

"What?"

"People deserving love."

She stopped and thought for a second. Fork down and all.

"Well...don't they?"

"Yeah, sure. It's just a weird thing to say about everyone."

"I'm just wishing them the best. Just like you. You haven't dated anyone in quite a while."

It was unlike her to bring up my love life. We didn't discuss the men who couldn't keep up with me over the years. I'd become fine with it.

"There's no one to date, Mom."

"There's half a world."

"Nope." A mental Rolodex of men who never understood me rolled through my head. Each face with a giant, red X on it. "Plus, I think you know I've been a little busy."

"Well, you look great."

Yes, because that's what counts.

"You're one to talk, Mom. There's half a world for you, too," I said, my tone sharp.

The women in my family were famously manless. My mother spoke of my father once, when I asked her who he was and why he was gone. We hadn't mentioned him again.

My mother's father had left her and Josephine when she was five years old, for another woman.

My grandmother's dad died in a war before she could ever meet him. Her mother raised her alone too, finally remarrying long after Josephine was grown and gone.

"*My mother always said that she had men after her, but she would never let another man finish what my father started. So she did it alone,*" my grandmother told me once, reminiscing about her own childhood. I guessed that was where it all started, my own run-ins with elusive romance. It was in my blood -- spelled out in the branches of a family tree infused with estrogen and mothers. But if anyone deserved love, I couldn't imagine a soul who should have been in line before Kim.

"So what about you, Mom?"

"What about me?"

"Do you deserve love?"

Her brown face turned bright pink and she giggled incessantly, looking around the dining room as if anyone else were there with us. What a show.

"What? Why are you asking me that?"

"You really brought it up. I just got to thinking when the last time you had some love was. And not in that gross way that I don't want to hear about."

"Well, it's been a while," she humbled, "but, I just don't have time for anybody right now."

"Why? What do you do?"

"I do a lot, daughter, thank you. And you will see that while you're here. I'm in classes, I volunteer, I have my garden out there. I mean -- a man? Really? Can you imagine? Where would he even fit?"

"Right next to you," I jokingly pointed to the large, empty seat next to her.

She feigned exhaustion of me. Or, maybe it was real.

"Oh please, it'll happen when the time is right," she sighed.

"Well, do you want it? Would you like a partner?"

"You make it sound like a lesbian!"

"What's lesbian about that?"

"Partner. You make it sound like Ellen."

"Oh my god. Mom," my entire head and eyeball set rolled. "Enough. All couples are partnerships. Ellen has a WIFE."

"Oh. Well, I think having a 'partner'," she used the biggest air quotes ever. Like full on bear paws, "would be nice. I have a lot of stuff around here that needs to be fixed, I'd like to have someone take me out to dinner. You know."

"Yeah, I know."

Mom looked down at her plate. Was she wistful? I reached across the table and grabbed her hand.

"Kim, you deserve love."

"Stop it. Don't mock me."

"I am totally fucking serious."

She smiled and shrugged.

"Thank you. I don't like that language."

That night, after falling asleep on the sofa with Mom, midway through an old William Holden movie, I climbed sleepily up the stairs and into my room, feeling all too familiar. Yes, many years removed me from this place, but if the constraints of time hadn't existed, it could have been fifteen years earlier. I could have been a teenager. And JC Chasez could have been the love of my life.

I stood in the doorway, taking in the room again. It was small. How did I ever grow so big in it? I always felt so much bigger than this room, or house, or city. Like I couldn't be contained, though everything tried its damnedest to reign me in. Make me take solace in the normal. I was never comfortable in that.

I was Alice through the looking glass, and Omaha was full of oddities I didn't understand. Comfort zones and manageable thoughts and opinions. I drank the potion, and my legs shot out through the windows and my head through the roof, my arms the size of Boeings. The whole town shouting, "Off with her head."

I sat on the bed and bounced. I wondered if it remembered my body shape and would invite me back in with a wide open welcome and supportive springs.

Across from the bed, on top of the tube TV, was a memory board.

"Holy shit," I whispered.

I thought I had thrown that thing out forever ago. Mom salvaged everything; I should have known. It was covered in pictures, ticket stubs, pins, notes, stickers.

Stickers. Where did you even buy stickers anymore? I leaned in further to discover this treasure trove of a past life.

God, I was skinny. And I didn't even try, I never tried, and I was never thin enough.

God, those huge fucking glasses. Of course, now they were in style, and every hipster in town wanted a pair that I and other nerds paved the way for. Those shirts with built-in bras and spaghetti straps. Those damn wedge platforms. That damn blue eyeshadow. Why hath thou forsaken me, early aughts?

There was a picture of Stassi and I both sitting in tubs pulling each other's hair. It was the night of my first fight with Shep, and we played stupid games to keep my spirits up. Thought the world was coming to an end.

Shepherd and me at one of those radio station concerts. The ones with fifteen fledgling bands and a washed-up host. He was freezing, so I wrapped my sweater around him. Six foot three, 250 pounds, wearing a gray cable knit underneath a parasol with no

shame. I wore a tank top and cargo pants and jumped in the mosh pit and touched hands with lead singers, occasionally bringing him back Dippin' Dots. That was our purest essence. We had been inseparable, alter egos of each other.
Teenage clichés.

I remembered the shifts that happened gradually that led us to who we were going to be. The red flags that waved along the way that one day it wouldn't be like that. There was always a tectonic plate inside of me threatening to quake and destroy.

# 3

## Alex

I pulled my running shoes out of a dark corner of my bag and strapped them on, feeling relief when I saw red, Austin clay in the crevices.

It wasn't a dream. I had actually been there.

I tightened the laces around my short socks and did a stretch before pounding the pavement in my old neighborhood. The old neighborhood, where everything was just how I left it, but me. The first leg of a run out of Mom's house was either straight uphill or toward a main street. I opted for the hill, hoping to disappear into the quiet rows of family homes. Large, historic Tudors made of brick and perfectly manicured lawns.

Three houses up, Mrs. Landon was in her yard with her hat and gloves, up with the sun. I quickly threw a hand up to acknowledge her and was gone before she could have recognized me. The rain the night before made way for a fantastic morning smell. Earthworms and muddy leaves raked into large, wet piles, surprised by the shower.

I turned right at the top of the hill, a shortcut into the bricked-street back alleys of historic North Omaha. A place known nationwide for shootings and gangs, which I knew for peaceful morning runs and mediocre pot, if you wanted it.

The path I was running had no sidewalks. Just bumpy, uneven streets with large curbs on either side, and hills. The chain-link fence that used to house a Rottweiler was the chain-link fence that housed a new German Shepherd. Rose bushes became azaleas, sand boxes became starter cars, and grills were still on front porches.

I twisted up an unused circle of pavement. At the top was an overlook with a panorama and a glimpse of the meager downtown skyline. I sat on a bench, feet in the seat for a wider view and said hi to my first Omaha autumn morning in god knew how long. Pricked with the cooling sweat underneath my jacket, it was just how I remembered October being.

Crisp and damp. Something somewhere smelling of fire. A hint of wintertime.

A heavy, blue Buick came driving up the street behind me, bumping loud music and selling that so-so pot I was talking about. I flagged them down.

"Oh my goodness, you scared me," Mom clung to her chest when I came back into the house, half an hour later. I took a leisurely pace coming back so I could air out any skunky smell I might have been carrying.

"Why?"

"Well, I woke up and you were just gone. No note, your phone was here. I should've known you went out running. I just thought --"

"What? You thought I'd been raptured?"

"What is that? Is that the thing with the clothes being left behind? I heard that was a prank."

"It is, Mom," I sneaked past her and poured myself a tall glass of filtered water. Nebraska's tap water was among the worst drinking water in the nation, so I took the same precautions here as I did in Mexico, until they got it together.

"I drink the water here, and I'm fine," Mom had told me over the phone when I warned her about it.

"No, you're not fine; the chemicals just make you complacent enough to think you're fine. And that's what they want," I surmised onto deaf ears. Watching her drink from the tap made me cringe. But what did I know about health and safety, anyway?

"Well, how was your run?"

"Needed. Everything is just where I remember it. God, from the news I thought I'd be coming home to a war zone."

"They have to get their gang bang stories. You know it's always been quiet on this side."

"Yeah. Mom, don't say gang bang."

Although I knew the other side of the North O media sensation, it didn't stop me from worrying about her living alone. I bought her a security system a couple years back. She tripped the alarm so many times herself, the police told her they'd do extra patrol on her block if she'd get rid of it.

Mom was always good at making friends like that.

"How are you feeling?" she asked for the first time of many.

"I feel great, Mom. I'm going to go take a shower."

"What are your plans today?"

"Nothing really. I kind of just want to bum around your house if you don't mind."

"I don't. You can do that. I have a couple of church meetings this morning, but I'll come back to make you lunch."

"Sounds good."

I stepped out of the shower to a ringing cell phone and made no quick attempt to get it. I thought about shutting it off altogether: one of those times when you wanted to disappear and have everyone forget who you were, that they ever knew you, and become as anonymous as a newborn baby. Only your mother cared that you existed.

There was no one I had a need to connect with. Not even *need*. I didn't have a moderate *want* to connect, just a full-fledged yen to vanish. Anonymity was impossible without someone thinking you were dead or depressed.

Three missed calls. Alex.

I threw the phone back on the bed, wondering what could be so important. I was sure he was being dramatic. I hadn't called or texted when I landed last night as promised. He thought I was landing in a cornfield somewhere, not in a city of nearly a million.

Alexandr Clinton was my best friend.

We had clung tight to each other since our sophomore year in college at UT. We both dropped out and refused to go back to our respective homes, Omaha and Atlantic City.

We'd shared phone numbers, whiskey bottles, beds, dreams, apathy, colds, secrets, and a deep well of pure, unadulterated, raw life. The kind of life you shared when you had the dangerous freedom of being completely accepted for everything you were and weren't. We had that.

We were business partners, running a successful photography company. Cohabitors, sharing our collaborative dream house. An old, married couple who forgot how to be intimate, and who weren't married. Old friends with nowhere to hide.

For that reason,, I didn't want to answer his call. He knew me too well, and when you wished to be no one, that could really mess up the plan.

A text rang through.

*Seriously?* it said.

I rolled my eyes, knowing he could tell that I had read it. I sighed -- fine.

*I'm safe. I'm home. I'll call you later.*

I lied, but it was a good lie. Buying him peace of mind and me peace and quiet, at least for now.

I lay across my bed, still wrapped in my towel. I stared at the popcorn ceiling, which had a dusty fan attached to it.

It was 100 degrees in Texas. Sweltering hot and humid, sticky like sugar water gathering fruit flies. Our Texas house was tiled, designed to keep you cool when the sun couldn't care less. Smooth terracotta floors in traditional ranch-style architecture. Arched doorways and open showers.

There was nothing like it in either Omaha or Atlantic City. The house was built around a courtyard patio that Alex and I filled with plants and furniture and fountains for our hidden adult oasis. We decided to buy the house together four years before, after another bad falling out with another shitty landlord. We realized that we were -- for the foreseeable future -- stuck together. Hetero life mates.

He was worried and upset and probably hungry. It was very last minute when I sprung it on him that I was leaving for Omaha for an indeterminate amount of time. He had supported me, for the most part, and then, in the final minutes before my flight, had a total breakdown.

"Where is everything?" he said, suddenly panicked.

"What everything?"

"Everything in the house. I don't know where you put shit. What if I need vinegar?"

"It's above the fridge. What would you need it for?"

"I don't know. I don't know. What the hell do you use vinegar for?"

"Cleaning. Eating. You can make salad dressing. Alex, what are you talking about? You do all the cooking. You know about the vinegar."

"See? What the fuck?" he was shaking his head sadly from side to side. "Fuck" was a word that had been missing from his vocabulary for a long time, as he replaced his party-boy lifestyle with finer things and stronger language. I knew he was cracking.

"Are you okay?" I patted and rubbed his back, comforting him.

"Why do you have to go back to Omaha? This shit just really..." he trailed off. "I don't think you should go. I don't want you to go."

"You're gonna come up and see me. I'll see you in a week?"

"And then what?"

"And then I don't know, Al. I don't know. I'll take you to the zoo."

"It's gonna be cold."

"It's mostly inside, anyway."

"I have a lot of work to do. So it may be longer than a week. I have to train the intern. I have to --"

"I know your schedule. I built it."

"Okay, so you know."

"Yeah."

He was still sulking but begrudgingly accepted my invitation to the zoo. The promise of a baby hippo could fix anything. If you ignored the fact that they were captive.

Alex had wanted to road trip the fourteen-hour drive north together; we had taken so many road trips, he thought it seemed right. I just wanted to get there. I didn't want to stop at truck stops and play games and sing over each other listening to the Pixies. I didn't want that much enjoyment. Just drop me off in the cornfield, Alex; I'd be fine.

# 4

## Here We Go

*Hey, I'm home.*

I sent the text out, not really wanting to start a conversation. It was an informational thing.

Hey, I'm home. Okay. Please know that, but leave me alone.

Was it possible to be passive-aggressive to yourself? Because I was.

I thought I would come to Mom's house and melt into the furniture and become a television vegetable. I realized after four days that I was as easily bored as ever. There were only so many Marlon Brando movies I could watch before *The Godfather*-era, and then I lost interest. The incredible ridiculousness of daytime TV had never done it for me. I had to be in a bad way to watch a baby-daddy saga.

I caught myself drooling at an episode of *Maury*, actively hating the commercials because I wanted to know the test results. A personal rock bottom. I needed to get out. So that's when I reached out to Shep and Stassi.

Stassi was the first to respond, *Hey! Awesome, I didn't know you were coming.*

*Surprise.* I wanted that text to sound weary; I didn't think it worked like that.

*Let's meet up.*

Oh. It was a Tuesday afternoon; I figured she'd be working. Or busy with the kids or PTA or something.

*How's 4?*

I checked the time. It was 2:30. She really meant it.

*Okay.*

A wave of spit-swallowing anxiety raced over me. I wasn't ready to see people. Why did I text? Why was nothing ever good enough for me? My mind yelled, pacing back and forth up there. Why couldn't you just enjoy Maury Povich like everybody else? Now you have to meet up, catch up, answer questions. We hate questions! Especially from *her*.

I exhaled in an attempt to quiet myself. It was going to be okay. *She sounded excited to see you*, said a much calmer, more British, voice of reason. It would be good to catch up.

Yes. It would. I hadn't seen Stassi in nearly three years. Although we kept in touch via texts and Facebook, our friendship had changed. It felt increasingly forced between us. A small symptom of our teenage life together grew larger with time and space and age. We had become vastly different people with disparate philosophies, patterns, and motivations. There had always been evidence of those differences, but they were more sever.

The types we'd become.

As teenagers, I felt a thirst for competition emanating from Stassi, lurking beneath the surface. She had a knack for the subversive, teenage-girl mindfucks we watched movies about. Things like copying my outfits down to the shoes. "Discovering" something I'd introduced her to weeks before. Telling me things she'd heard said about me then begging me not to confront the person. Things that seemed like petty teenage crap but, when bolstered into adulthood unchecked, were vicious. Very *Single White Female.*

Obviously, I thought Stassi had her good points. She was funny sometimes, she would always help you clean, pack, hang a picture, or bake something. She knew when to not drive after drinking. Those things made for a great friend. But mostly, anymore, we were just habit.

At four o'clock that afternoon, I was sitting across from Stassi Hupp, nėe Whitaker, in the booth of a German Bier Haus. I wasn't going to choose that day to have my personal ire with Stassi come to a head. I tried to lead with the good things and braced for the worst. I never stopped having hope for the friendship.

Stassi sat across from me; her blonde hair was curly, framing her wide, red smile and bright blue eyes. She had a crooked nose with a slightly bulbous end, permanent bags under her eyes, and gapped teeth. She carried herself as better looking than she was, and that said something. I supposed if someone described the bare mechanics of my face, I wouldn't be that pretty, either.

Long face, flat nose, gummy smile.

"Have you ever been here?" she asked, leaning in. I didn't remind her that I was the one who introduced her to this place centuries ago; I just nodded and sipped.

"I have."

"I love this place. We come here every Wednesday with Aaron's friends. Well, our friends."

"Fun," I said, though I'd rather spend a night eating my feet than spend a night with Stassi's husband's overly opinionated, loud-mouthed crew, who just happened to know everything about everything. She didn't invite me, so that didn't matter.

"So, how does it feel to be back? You've missed so much."

"I have. Umm, it feels good to be back," I lied through a pained grin. "It's good to be here?" I answered and asked all at once.

"Yeah, I'm so surprised. You didn't let on."

"It was very last minute."

"Have you seen Shep yet?"

"Nope. No. I was thinking of surprising him tomorrow."

"Okay, I won't tell him you're here then."

"Thanks."

"And you HAVE to see my girls."

"Oh my god, they're so big."

"SO BIG. I mean, you've never even met Irie."

"No, I know. I want to. I wish you could have brought them here! Are they in day care?"

"Yeah. I had the day off, but when I heard from you I thought I'd just take them over there."

"Oh, you should have brought them! That'd be so fun," I said, realizing I had never dined with a small child.

Stassi looked at me as though my hair had caught on fire.

"You don't bring kids into bars," she said deliberately.

"There are always kids in bars in Texas. This place is totally empty, and it serves food."

She closed her eyes and shook her head. "That's so inappropriate."

I reached for the menu stuffed inside a Miller Lite six-pack package and pointed to the back page.

"They have a kids menu."

"No."

She pursed her lips and bobbled her head no, over and over.

"Alright, alright. We could also have gone somewhere else."

I put the menu back and wondered where we went from there.

"It's a good thing you're not having kids, I'd feel so bad for them," she said, dismissively, with a laugh. I started to go for it, but I didn't exactly get it.

"What?"

"It's just not a lifestyle for you. I mean, you would bring your kids into a bar? That's not how parenting works."

"Well, I don't know what I would do, but I think every parent has their own style. And as long as your kid is taken care of and loved -- you know..."

"No. There are a million different ways to screw up your kids. And taking them into a bar is probably number one. Just trust me. You don't know until you have one. Which you won't, so..."

"Okay."

It stung, but I dropped it. She had no idea.

"So, why are you here? Are you staying?" Stassi seemed as eager as I was to talk about something else. Although, I would have picked anything but that topic, too. The weather: people didn't talk about the weather, anymore.

"Umm, I'm here -- just because. I don't know how long I'm staying. It is so nice out today. Isn't it?

"Yeah. You don't know how long you're staying? I never thought I'd see you back here indefinitely."

"I know it. Me either. I forgot how unpredictable Nebraska is. It was freezing yesterday; today, it's t-shirt weather."

"Is everything okay? You're not running away from heartbreak are you?"

I nearly spat out my beer.

"No, no. Not at all. I'd be so lucky."

"Yeah, you haven't been with anyone since --"

"A lifetime. It's been a lifetime. But, it's fine, I've been able to just focus on my career, and that's paying off."

"Oh yeah...your picture-taking thing."

"Photography. Yes."

"I think it's so cute people still get by with the arts. Good for you."

"Yeah -- we, get by."

"Oh right, you and Alex. That's his name, right?"

"Yeah, Alex."

I'd been talking about him for fifteen years now; despite that, Stassi had met Alex twice. With ample opportunity to engage with him more than that, Stassi had made her mind up about him long before.

"I don't know about him," Stassi asserted, as though that meant anything.

"Know what about him? I could tell you anything you need to know."

"I don't know, sometimes he makes me uncomfortable."

"You've met him twice; when would sometimes be?"

I felt my mouth turn sour in defense.

"His Facebook just gives off that troubled vibe. Like a loner, or something."

"Alex is one of the most well-adjusted, self-aware people I've ever met."

"He's always posting those weird odes and showing off his tattoos. I don't know. I just look at those and wonder if he's crying for help."

"What odes?" I was growing hotter, rapidly.

"Like that one about a cat and a tree...I don't know. I know that being in the trees is code for pot. Is that legal down there now?"

"No, it's still Texas."

"I guess drug use would make sense."

"Alex doesn't do drugs. And those words are Cure lyrics, not odes."

"What is that? A band?"

"Yeah, it's the Cure."

"I don't know them."

"Well, you don't know Alex, either. And that's too bad."

"I mean, I guess you know him better than me. It's just the vibe that I get."

"I don't think your vibe compares to my decade and a half of friendship, Stassi."

"Right, of course. Gosh, has it been that long already?"

"Yeah. We're fast-tracking to forty, believe it or not."

Again our conversation was diffused, as though no tension was ever shared.

"I never thought I'd see you with short hair." Stassi referenced my head. My fingers lifted to touch the pieces, still growing in.

"Yeah, I know." I said insecurely.

"I found my first gray hair," she leaned in and whispered. "It was on the side."

I felt silly, but my heart really did skip a beat at this confession and my annoyance lessened.

"Okay, so I'm back in Weight Loss Extreme, did I tell you that? I mean, it's my fourth time trying it. And you know, I have some success and then something happens, and I blow up again. So now, I'm trying to work out more. I think if I just added a little more activity to what I'm doing it'll really stick this time."

I interject with an "Mm-hm."

"So I've been taking a SpiritCycle class. Have you heard of these?"

"I think so?"

"It's like spiritual cycling. And, you know I'm about as spiritual as a shopping mall," she said, and I snorted up some beer in a surprised chuckle.

"But honestly, I read one of those silly things you posted about feelings and health and then I saw this SpiritCycle was coming to Omaha, and I thought I'd go try it."

"And?" I furthered her, intrigued.

"And the class was really hard, and I could barely breathe, but there were other people way bigger than me in there, and I sat in the back. But, anyway," she slowed down again. "I leave class, and I'm just dripping sweat, and I'm looking in the mirror, which they tell you to do afterward. I pull my hair back, and there she is."

I almost asked who, having forgotten where this story started.

"A thick white hair. Prominent and screaming at me. I almost had a heart attack right then and there."

There was a time that was the biggest nightmare we could have imagined. Give us a gun, load up the bullets, and kiss your life goodbye.

"I plucked it out and wrapped it in a napkin for evidence."

"Evidence of what?"

"For my stylist. I thought I'd seen one before and it was just the poor lighting I was in, but this one -- was the real thing. So we colored it this color;" she referenced her several blonde tones and emphasized, with very precise mouthing, "we're getting old."

"Yeah. Yeah," I slowly mused.

"Can you imagine? Wrinkles, gray hair. My grandmother is ninety-eight years old, do you know what that does to the body?"

"I can imagine."

"I can't. There is nothing worse than getting old. What a nightmare."

# 5

## Becky
## (And Other Musings)

I had this friend back in Austin.

Her name was Becky -- a complete and polar departure from everything she was. A person whose name absolutely abandoned the structure of her personality but whose personality filled the name out to its edges so well that she was undeniably Becky. Bursting at the seams, Becky.

Becky was an amputee ballet instructor and Girl Scout leader. She had one arm, the left one, and she had taught herself how to write with it, being naturally right-handed. Her arm was missing from beneath the elbow, so there was still a bend to it. She covered the whole of it with a beautiful, rooted tree that twisted into a full-on garden sprouting from her back, drawing attention to the missing forearm and hand, and distracting from it, as well.

When she was fifteen, she was in a cataclysmic car accident; she lost her sister in it and almost her mother, too. Her arm had been mangled, and they couldn't save it, so they took it. Becky had always told me that if I had met her then, I wouldn't have thought for one second that she was the same person.

She said that other than losing her sister and her arm -- two incredible tragedies that I couldn't fathom -- she had lost her identity.

The person she had been all those fifteen years. Beautiful and carefree and vain. Her sister and she were both gorgeous, leggy, girl-next-door-meet-Kardashian types. They were made up, styled, coached, and staged like prized purebreds and raised in a privileged home that delighted in their pageantry. Both in flippers, wigs, eyelashes, and heels since they were two.

Becky's sister, whose name she never mentioned, had been Miss Teen Texas with big hopes of going all the way. Becky's mom had been Miss Texas 1982 and when that didn't work out for her, she gunned for and won Miss Mom Texas 1994. Becky followed them in everything from beauty regimen to the grand plan for one of the Holland girls to become a Texas champion.

Ms. America. Ms. USA. The world.

They were beautiful, they were adored, they were invincible, she said.

Becky's mom had been putting on mascara and talking on the car phone; she didn't see the stop sign or the tractor-trailer from the right. Becky's sister wasn't wearing her seatbelt, and Becky remembered it was because she didn't want to wrinkle the silk shirt she was wearing. It had ruffles in front, and they were going to meet her new coach. Her mother agreed, saying they were only going right up the street.

Becky wasn't wearing her seatbelt, either, but was thrown from the rear of the car and into the gravel road, missing the brunt of the damage. The car was totaled, twisted and bent into an unrecognizable pile of what could have been anything. They used the Jaws of Life to pull out Becky's mom, whose legs pinned her next to her dying daughter for over half an hour. Becky said her mother and she were changed in every way after that. Irrevocably damaged and forever altered.

When I thought of feeling sorry for myself, I thought of Becky. I thought of climbing inside her soul and seeing what strength and sorrow actually looked like. Because I'd never experienced anything close to that, and I didn't think I would be able to handle it. I considered myself a strong person, but if you were only as strong as your experience allowed, at the time I had nothing in comparison. I thought about Becky when I saw pretty girls with no worries and when I saw homeless veterans wheeling around, looking for the handouts they were owed. She was somewhere firmly juxtaposed between, and I found it odd and awesome to know anyone who could span that gap.

Becky had to teach herself to walk again. She had detached vertebrae, and her mother and she were both in therapy for over a year afterward. Her mother barely spoke for that first year, a stark contrast to the person she knew as her mom. A traditional Southern woman with stories, and hospitality for days.

Becky turned to her oldest love, dance, for inspiration to keep pushing the boundaries of her injuries and learn to move again. Not just move -- dance, and just a few years ago, she became an instructor for little girls with big dreams.

Becky had almost buzzed hair, close to her face. It left her eyes as the focal point. They were round, brown vessels of emotion. They were still so bright and innocent. I searched them when she told me this story; I didn't know what I was looking for -- damage, I guessed. All I saw was truth...and hope. She wore them brimmed with mascara and black liner and was usually smiling. She carried her sister's picture on her chest, in magnificent black and gray, and talked about it in tattoo terms.

"If I'm going to get a portrait done, I'm only doing it in Austin, New Orleans, or LA; they're the only ones who know what the hell they're doing. In the states, anyway. I have seen some really busted-up faces on a portrait. Have you seen some of these things? They don't even look like people. They've got these wet, paper-bag faces, and I'm just like, that can't be your mom's face. I look at the person who has the tattoo, I look at the tattoo and back and forth. And I'm just like, that can't be your mom's face, because she looks like a wet paper bag and you look like a person, and I think you should get your money back, you know? I searched and researched for the right person to do my sister's face. She was so beautiful that it had to be perfect, just like she'd want it. I felt militant when I went and got it. Like I had a gun to their head and if they missed one line or shadow -- boom! They'd be done. You have to have a lot of trust for someone to tattoo you, you know? I mean, it's my sister. It's my arm. Like, I'm naked, I'm the bottom of how raw a person can get, and I'm just giving me to you. All these precious parts of me, I'm just going to hand them over to a stranger to color. That takes so much trust. And -- and vulnerability. But I'm happy with it; I love having her so close, and I would trust my artist with my life. I really would."

I thought about Becky's sister, feeling sorry for myself and wanting to snap out of it. When I thought of her, I felt no right to devastation. She had never made it past seventeen. I was ancient compared to her. If thirty-three years was a lifetime then wow. Wow. Wow. Wow.

# 6

## Shepherd

SHEP WAS MY FIRST LOVE.

Not my first crush or even my first kiss but my first the-world-is-ending-stay-up-late-talking-pregnancy-scare-heartbreak-break-up first love.

To see the two of us together, you wouldn't have known we spoke the same language. My bronze-colored skin, his pale, freckled face. My aqua hair, his military-short, red buzz. My Van Halen t-shirt and leggings, his Old Navy fleece.

He was built to be the high school quarterback with the personality of the class clown. He was funny. In high school. He was all poop jokes and monkey farts. Sweet, cherubic innocence radiated out of his open, generous heart. After that, he was misguided, complacent, and perpetually not living up to his potential.

I had warned him about this. For years before it mattered. Striving to help him find something, anything, that he loved nearly as much as poop jokes and monkey farts.

I never had the will to live in my town and work my job and just know people I already knew. But my friends did. Shep championed this. He had his schedule down. The routine right. None of it actually involved doing things. It took me a long time to accept that as any sort of life worth living. I still struggled with it. It could be easier to see the greatness within others and not your own. For years, I had seen the greatness in Shepherd, with no way of making him see it himself. That was a chief factor in my decision to leave Omaha and never look back. His unwillingness to thrive. To fly away with me. He had so many excuses and not enough reasons.

But I couldn't deny -- Shepherd was the best boyfriend.
We dated for two years and three months. He was kind, attentive, and patient, and he never brought me flowers. Back when I was a sullen teenager, flowers reeked of that unoriginal, corporate love that I just couldn't be bothered with. I was different. I wanted to be treated differently. So he had brought me geodes, dinosaur toys, nerdy tokens of his affection that made my heart soar with "he gets me."
In high school, Shep did theater. He should have been an actor. And I would have never said that about anyone.
I thought most people who said they were an actor were really saying they were an emotionally unstable person with attention-seeking behavior who lied a lot, slept around, waited tables, and lived at home, but it was okay because their parents believed in them, and they were going to make it one day.
I heard the word actor and walked the other way. We were not going to be friends. You were going to quote movies.
But Shepherd, and maybe it was my childhood sentiments doing the thinking, Shepherd was an amazing and dedicated actor. If I could have just dug up the VHS tapes thrown somewhere in

our parents' basements. Damn. I mean, I remembered this kid, and he was so good, he could make you laugh and cry in one show. I helped him run lines and would get lost, utterly taken by his delivery, his command. That was how you fell in love as a teenager. One of the tall boys talked good.

"You should pursue this," I egged him on, one night between high school and college.

"Maybe."

"What are you going to go to school for?"

"Not theater! That's a dead end. There's no future in that."

"Then what else? You like math. Math?"

"Hell no. I don't know. I don't want to think about it too much; it'll come to me. Right now, I just want to focus on this show and you. I mean, things are going really well at the movie theater, they're talking about promoting me."

"What -- that's amazing!"

"I'm not going to take it if they do. It's just nice they want to."

"Why wouldn't you take that?"

"I don't want the responsibility of management. I'm happy where I am, and they need me there."

"In the ticket booth."

"Sometimes I do concessions."

I hadn't talked to Shepherd in over a year or seen him in longer. We texted sporadically, but I always felt we were trying to hold on to the friendship that we used to have that we had both outgrown. We didn't understand each other's lives anymore. I guessed we didn't have to. The most we had in common was shared history.

I stepped up in line, and he was looking at the monitor screen, not noticing me.

"Can I get the new Adam Sandler movie, for one, please?"

His face immediately twisted, perturbed, before he saw me.

"Adam Sandler hasn't done a movie --" he looked up. "Hey!"

Shepherd's face and dimples lit up. Young looking as ever, his hair with mottled gray on the sides.

"Holy shit, you're here."

"Hi! Can you come out?"

"Yeah, yeah."

It took him a few moments to come around to the lobby. When he did, he scooped me up in a tight bear hug and kissed my crown, like he'd always done.

"Hi, bud!" I said, reaching my forearms as far around as they would go under his hug.

"Look at this hair," he scruffed me. "What are you doing in town?"

"I'm here for a while. I'm staying with my mom."

"Are you moving back?"

"No, god no," I said out of habit, not knowing if that was the real answer. I did that often, sounding more adamant than I really was.

"Yeah, I couldn't see you coming back here for good. The city would fall apart."

"Yeah. Well then, maybe. Maybe I'll be back," I shrugged in a weak attempt to correct myself.

"I'm off at nine. Wanna go to Village Inn?"

I laughed.

"Village Inn?"

"I am craving pancakes. I was going to go by myself. Unless you want to get a drink."

"No -- no, pancakes sound great. I, uh, I took a cab out here, if you can take me home."

"Of course. Yeah. Awesome, I'll be right back."

I spent the next ten minutes wandering around the lobby of the theater. They had made some aesthetic updates in the past fifteen years, but it was mostly the same. Same bright/funky color palette and graphic carpet that was stapled into theaters across the world.

Same pimply, pubescent kids working behind the concessions counter. God, I had spent hours in that building.

Those early, teenage-relationship days before you discovered sex or drinking -- spent in dark movie theaters with sweaty hands and the sweet illusion of freedom. Sometimes we spent the whole day in dark theaters. Shep would map the start times perfectly, and I would happily go along, skipping from movie to movie with him. It was so simple. I thought we'd get married and have kids. How fucking weird.

Me and Shepherd? Together forever? It was hilarious to think about. Where would we have lived? What would we have done? I never thought that if I wanted to see Shep, he'd be in the same place I'd left him. I supposed I wasn't surprised. In some ways, it was a success. He found something that made him happy, and he stuck with it. It had taken me years to find what made me happy, and I was searching for more. So in that way, he was ahead of the game. Wasn't that what most people were searching for? What made them happy?

No one ever said it couldn't be a near twenty-year stint at the movie theater ticket booth.

"I'm doing this new thing," Shep whispered to me, piquing my interest.

"Okay," I said, bending over the Formica table between us.

"So, okay, you know how, like, when we go to the movies, I get us comp tickets?"

"Yeah, of course."

"So, those tickets aren't tracked. I don't know how this got overlooked, but it's not tracked in the computer system whether I take them out or if they're accounted for or anything."

"Wow, that's a huge flaw."

"I know."

I got excited and immediately guilty. I should never have thought poorly of Shepherd staying at the theater. I underestimated him. He saw a problem, and he was going to solve it. A ticket-tracking program could have been huge. Every theater in America could have used one.

"So who's your developer?" I asked, cutting him off.

"What do you mean?"

"For the ticketing software. Like, who's helping you do it? I know some great guys. Austin is chock-full of web guys."

"No. What?"

His whole face scrunched up in confusion. We were both confused, looking at each other over stacks of pancakes and a chocolate milkshake.

"No. I take the comp tickets and give them to people, but I still take their money and pocket it."

I sat there quietly, trying to comprehend what he was saying and why he was so proud of it.

"You give them free tickets," I started slowly.

"Mm-hm."

"And then they pay you regular price, and then you keep the money."

"Yup," he nodded, smiling, very nonchalant about the fact that he was an --

"Embezzler? Shepherd, really? That's embezzlement or extortion or what?"

"It's twenty thousand more dollars this year."

"What?"

I leaned even farther across the table.

"You made twenty thousand extra dollars?"

"Yup."

His lips pursed in a proud expression, and his eyes lit up like he was telling me about vacation or a newborn.

"How long have you been doing this?"

"Three years now."

"Three years?!" I whisper-yelled. "Why haven't you told me? Are you scared to get caught?"

"Not really. There's, like, no way I can get caught. I have two guys working under me now, and they're sworn to secrecy. That's why I've kept it hush. No one knows but you."

"Working under you? Like a pyramid scheme?"

"Of sorts. Ponzi-esque."

Shepherd was reminding me of those people who played with lightsabers. Like they knew it was just a toy and this was all play, but deep down inside their reality/fantasy switch was skewed. So they thought fighting with lightsabers was more important than it really was. Then they went and shot up a mall. It was all very "dark web".

"Those guys cover the times that I'm not working so that it doesn't come back to just my shifts. If it ever does come back, which it won't. And they give me a percentage of what they make."

"Do you give them a percentage of yours?"

"No. No way; I'm the leader. My cut to them is keeping my mouth shut."

"What if one of them blows this? What happens?"

Shepherd tut-tutted and shook his head.

"They wouldn't. They're too scared. I have ways of handling things."

Who said things like that? Mob bosses and guys with too many episodes of something on VHS.

"What does that mean?"

"They just wouldn't cross me."

I pushed my plate away from me and tried to find my footing.

"Okay, so why are you doing this? I'm not -- I'm not trying to judge you; I guess I just don't get it."

"Well. For the money."

"Okay. So why don't you just not work at the movie theater? Like, get a different job?"

I could have sworn that in that moment, I was talking to a second-chance teen and not a grown man. The strange thing was the tension I was starting to feel between us. We were genuinely not seeing each other's sides. I retracted everything I said earlier. About Shepherd maybe having found the secret to happiness in mediocrity. No, no -- this was what happened when you worked your teen job for twenty years. You completely fucking snapped.

"I'm really happy where I am. I love working at the theater. They wouldn't know what to do if I left, that place would go up in flames."

"Would it?"

"Oh, yes. YES. This is my way of getting paid what I'm actually worth to them. So they get to keep me, and I get a living wage."

"What do you make there? Legally?"

"Nine-fifty an hour."

"Holy shit. Even after all this time?"

"Yeah, the system just sets us up to fail. I thought you'd be more about this."

"Why?"

"Because you're always pulling sneaky shit. You were the one who told me 'You're only in trouble if you get caught.'"

I thought for a second about what in the hell he was referring to. I had definitely had my fair share of getting-my-way stories, but none of them involved felony-level crime sprees. It was more like walking into the zoo without paying. Or that time we got kicked off a playground for stealing sand for my beach birthday. I could have justified anything and everything with a passionately delivered speech and a call to arms. To Shepherd, there was no difference between the two.

I got it. I bet that was giving him a rush. That made him feel important. He was the boss over the boys working under him, and that was the most power he'd ever felt. After all these years, he was still acting, just in some depraved, real-life scenario. That was his

*Pygmalion.* I was supposed to be throwing roses onto the stage, not writing a scathing review. But I couldn't.

I was disappointed. I was: what the fuck?

I didn't want to get into any more particulars with Shepherd. I wanted to enjoy his company without knowing too much about his life. If a guy was openly and proudly extorting from his job, I didn't even want to think about his browser history.

"Shepherd," I started.

"Yeah."

"It's important for you to know, that's a line from Disney's *Aladdin.* I didn't make it up, I just said it to get what I wanted. 'You're only in trouble if you get caught.'"

"Either way. It changed my life. And, tonight's on me."

He paid the $10.95 in cold, hard, other people's cash.

Shep drove me back to my mom's house. I was sure he could have done that with his eyes closed. We'd spent so many drives together. Hours in cars, listening to *Lifehouse.* Or a soundtrack. Or nothing and just talking.

Our first fight was in a car, and I don't even remember what it was about, just that my heart was breaking and we were both crying. He first kissed me in a car, too. I thought maybe our last kiss was also in one. I didn't know that for certain.

Shepherd was still so innocent. The gilded gift of age, gray hair, the changing world -- nothing had tarnished this boyish naiveté he had always held. Even the world of crime. If I were a judge sitting across from him as he attempted to exonerate himself, I'd wrap him in a blanket and whisper that he should tell me all about it, like I would a child in a bad emotional state. Because even if the basics were black and white, wrong and right, something about him just didn't know that.

I was probably making excuses but that didn't mean they weren't true. Anyway, maybe he had a point. Maybe they did owe him

more than his measly paycheck. His twenty years of loyal service should have earned him far more than that. Nine-fifty? Who could have lived on that? How could they expect him to? The huge corporation didn't miss his twenty grand pay increase. So, maybe, I had judged too harshly. Maybe again, he had the secret.
I knew, if absolutely nothing else, his heart was gold. Tarnished. But gold.

We sat chatting more in his car after he had pulled into the long and cracked drive. We had more to talk about and catch up on than I'd expected. He asked me mostly about my opinion on movies and what I had seen recently. The list was short and unimpressive. He wrote things down for me to watch later.
I asked him about his mother, his father, and the gentrification of his part of town. Even our conversation harkened back to the old days.
Shep, light and current. Me, digging and prodding.
Shepherd had thinned out. His tall, soft body leaner than before. Broad shoulders more square, and his face more taut where the gravity was settling. He was handsome now. Not just cute. Not the chubby one, as people used to describe him -- to my fury.
And not over-the-top handsome, but if-you-look-long-enough handsome. I couldn't help but muse further about if we had stayed together. If the stars had aligned and the plan never changed. If we had been that teenage dream love story, what would we be doing now?
There was no way in hell Shepherd would still be working at the theater.
What would I have done? A whole life in the same city. I couldn't envision, even in my wildest imagination -- who I would have become. I supposed I would have sunk into the obscurity of small-city life.
Play dates and work anniversaries. Mom jeans and mom haircuts.

I would have slunk away into someone I would never recognize, dreams on hold, then thrown away. A whole life was a fantastical amount of time to become or unbecome someone.

On the other hand, maybe I would have thrived. A big fish in a little pond. Omaha was growing. Maybe I would have grown into it.

Maybe we could've been something special. I could've changed the course of his life with more than just a cartoon quote. I would've made him pursue his dreams and become someone tremendous.

I could have highlighted his potential and built us into a power couple. But -- I think I tried that. I think that was when I learned I only had enough breath for one.

I wished there was a What If app that could make thoughts like that more clear. Show you your parallel universe where all your questions were answered and lived out. Seeing where the grass was greener.

"Sorry," Shepherd interrupted my thoughts, laughing and waving his hand while reaching for the window. "I farted."

# 7

# The Legend of Blue Anise

Fifteen years ago, a girl named Jorah got on a plane and had big, big plans.

She was confident; she was cocky. She watched the skyline disappear underneath the clouds and didn't care if she ever saw it again. When she thought of her best friend and her boyfriend, they were already othered. They lived small where she took up space. They were meek where she was loud. They were comfortable where she was malcontent. She imagined she'd see them again one day, and they'd have nothing in common. And that was okay because the world was calling.

Six years later, I was a college dropout, living in Texas, operating a mechanical bull on Sixth Street. No shame, though. I was happy. Not the life-fulfillment, living-my-dreams, kind of happiness. But in the regularly drunk, size-six, lots-of-friends kind of happy. The deflecting kind. Two years into my general studies program at UT, I bombed.

If I thought Omaha was a trap, college was a straitjacket. I'd spent so long telling other people what they should be doing with their lives, I'd forgotten to turn the mirror onto mine. I couldn't even declare a major, for the love of Christ. So I did what any self-respecting college student would do -- took up partying and flunked out.

It wasn't hard to do: the parties were everywhere. The boys were everywhere. And the booze -- you know those first few times... it felt like magic. You felt like a superstar version of yourself, and everything was amped. I *loved* feeling amped. Amped to me was the equivalent of accomplished. If I wasn't doing shit, I was gonna be amped about it.

I met Alex on the cusp of that time. Over the transition from naive mid-western girl with passion, to Jorah, the Billy Goat of booze. He was in a similar place. He'd come there to go to law school. To get away from his hometown and to discover his life. What he discovered was he hated law, and as he'd always known, he wanted to be a photographer. So he was about to disappoint a lot of people in New Jersey, by denouncing a high-ranking profession and hiding behind the lens of what might have been artistic poverty.

We were barely twenty-one; we still counted our years in summers then. We fell in love hard and swift and out, nearly double. But our connection was undeniable, so our friendship was inevitable. We lived our lifestyles in tandem. And after long and close enough, I couldn't think of a me without him.

We were bitchy, irresponsible servers. We had hung out at the bars we worked at until way past close, drinking with our restaurant families. Sometimes, when shit hit the fan, we switched up quitting work in a firestorm. The one who stayed behind would float us both financially for the next two months. No hard feelings, the tide would soon turn. One didn't work without the other for long.

If you've ever been a server, you know how transitory the life can be.

"I have to get out of here, Brad is driving me crazy."
"He's on a power trip."
"I'm gonna quit tonight."
"Fuck it."
"This place will fall apart without me."
"Let it burn, bitch."
It'd take two more weeks to quit because there'd be double shifts we'd want to cash in on.

We were chain-smoking, kegger-throwing party monsters. Hosting loud and smoky parties in the basement of our rental house, packing it beyond safety with friends and strangers. Once a guy got stabbed and gave himself stitches in the bathtub. Once a girl beer-bonged thirteen Miller Lites in less than ten minutes. Okay, that was me.

We were professional, American nomads.
Every few months we'd get the wild hair and leave. We'd surprise each other and up and go. Telluride, because we could. Napa, because of wine. Mexico, because treat yourself. Eventually, those small vacations made way for longer trips. The summer we lived in an Airstream. The winter we left to work as ski lift operators. The six weeks we spent in Europe smoking pot and walking pilgrimages. The six-month stint in Central America volunteering for people who were better humans than anyone we knew stateside.
I loved that life with him. Sick, dirty, smelly, sad -- it didn't matter,

it was all okay. It was better than okay, it was the way it was supposed to be. No one in my life would have done those things with me, taken me to that level of discomfort. Let me take them to new heights of experience. Held hands and watched the world burn. He was everything I loved about myself, in a person I could hold.

That was where our real education was. Math: how long do we have to work until we can leave again? Geography: by foot or by fuel? Sociology: traveling with two Aussies, a Moroccan, and a Peruvian, who we still kept in touch with. Language: *mas vino por favor.* Law: "Officer, I assure you we are not carrying marijuana, but you'll need a warrant to search." General Studies: "Generally, I don't do this, but we have a connection, Giuseppe."

We were artists -- kind of.
Alex never went anywhere without his prized possession: his camera. He had a million pictures of me from those days. Younger and always, always laughing. Videos when I didn't know he was filming. Those photos covered our apartment. Well, not just of me, all of his subjects. Trees, a lot of trees. Empty playgrounds, old hands, abandoned alleys, relics of homes.

"You want to take some?" he asked me, walking through town one afternoon. He had been shooting building art. Painted brick.

"No way. I don't even know where to start, Al."

"It's easy. Come on."

He took his camera from around his neck and put it around mine. My skin bristled.

"Find something you like," he coaxed.

I looked around, it all just looked like town to me. Then I noticed a green bud in the sidewalk.

"That?" I pointed.

"Sure," he lifted the lens to my eye, and I peered through it.

The bud became bigger, the crack more pronounced.

"Once you like what you see, you push this button," he showed me.

"That's it?"

"Well, that's the beginning."

I snapped the button.

I looked at the picture. It was out of focus. But I was in love.

We were moonlighting freelancers and Austin was home base. We would balance restaurant work on nights and weekends and shoot whenever we could during the day. Sometimes Alex would get a "gig," and I'd assist him. It was the biggest deal ever. We'd bounce around the house, making up songs about living our dreams and everyone else was suckers.

"Fuck everyone who isn't us." The motto for getting paid $50 to take a headshot of someone's dog.

It was more of a hobby than a career move, and the call of the wild life was strong in both of us. Eventually, the cameras became dusty, without use. Our schedules filled to the brim with social gatherings and double shifts, time with the people we dated but didn't really like, and occasionally did. For all our revelations and evolutions we couldn't get out of our own way. We were happy, but we were stuck. Both. In the mud and wanting to drive out and into what was next for us.

"Maybe we should move," Alex brought up, "we need a change of city."

"No way. You know the rules. Nothing happens here that doesn't happen there."

"I do know those rules. They didn't apply to our hometowns... but I do know those rules."

"It's in here, Al," I touched my chest.

"In your bra?"

"Shut up. It's in here," I touched his chest.

"Ohh, in my bra."

Then, one day, a friend died.
When that happened it was like a light going off inside us. It was fucked the way that worked. You thanked the universe it wasn't you in that car, so you could still have time to change things. Redefine your purpose before it was your turn to go. Relocate the parts of you that you had lost.

Alex knew he wanted to be a photographer. He'd known that since he was five years old and armed with a viewfinder.
When I thought back to what I wanted to be, I didn't have anything like that. I had phases. I wanted to be a writer. I wanted to be a director. I wanted to be a journalist. But nothing that was in my blood rather than a passing obsession. I had more what-I-don't-want-to-bes than anything. The fulfillment from that wasn't sustaining.
I was in love with everything we'd done but still the restless girl at the core. I still needed more. I needed something purposeful and mine. Shooting dogs with Alex was fun...but it wasn't enough. Nothing ever was. And after Roxy died and all her dreams with her, I was hungry. I knew Alex was, too.

Blue Anise was named for the cocktails we were having when we decided to leave our jobs and start a company. We'd had quite a few of them and they were transformative. More than we knew.

"Don't you ever just want to -- UGH," I kicked my leg out and punched the air.

"All the fucking time," Alex slammed his drink down on the bar counter, ice cubes flying out.

"What happened to us, Al? We were going to do it. We were going to do it all. When did we give up?"

"We haven't given up. We've...we've..." he searched for the

word, staring ahead at the stocked bar. "Hey! Can we get two Jägerbombs? We haven't given up, J. We've conformed. We got caught in the cycle. And we're in the cycle right now."

"Oh my god. Oh my god," I panicked. The bar was spinning. I was twenty-six and had nothing to show for myself except I slept with the bartender and wasn't paying for shit.

"Don't lose it now," he comforted. Kind of. "If we could do anything, what would we do?"

"Travel."

"And to make money..."

"Ho? I don't know, Al!"

"No -- let's do it. Let's take pictures."

"For $50 a dog?"

"No. For our lives. Let's get serious about it. We've talked about this a hundred times."

It was true. We'd spent plenty of days daydreaming and what-iffing about it. But we never had a reason to jump into it.

"You think so?" I lifted my head from the bar top.

"I think we can do anything. Fucking everything."

"I WANT THAT," I whined so loud, sliding out of my seat. "I want that."

"Let's just jump in, J. We have each other."

I never forgot how earnestly he looked at me. A declaration in his eyes that no words could match. I knew I was safe. He knew the same.

So we never looked back.

At the time that I left, Blue Anise was the number one studio in Austin. We killed it on weddings. We traveled for people who fell in love with us but lived across the nation. We had shot weddings in India and Australia. We had freelanced in Giza and Rome.

We covered Ferguson and Baltimore, soothing our adrenaline-rush needs. We'd been featured in magazines across the world. And we had just celebrated the grand opening of Blue Anise - New Orleans. Turned out, I wasn't just a good photographer, I was pretty fucking good at sales and networking, too. We didn't even advertise anymore.

Blue Anise was the great adventure of my life.

# 8

## Getting High With Mom

The next morning I didn't have it in me to go on my run. The days were chilly and, lord, I hadn't been around cold air for most of my life at that point. My lungs begged for the humidity and sand of Texas. We missed the trails, the waterfront, the people. I really missed my people. My tribe. Back somewhere under the sun, where I belonged. Doing things I liked to do, without me. I was having a pity party.

I couldn't just come to Omaha and make new friends. You didn't really make new friends at my age. You made them before twenty-five and after fifty. Everything in-between you should have already had together.

Most people my age in Omaha were hidden behind the closed doors of their homes, raising children, and conducting marriages and businesses -- not trying to make friends. And neither was I. I didn't know what it was, but I'd sunk into the people and things I already knew. I didn't even seek out new music. I just loved what I loved. The people I didn't have to explain myself to, that I didn't have to retrace steps of my past to, for them to catch up. I liked it just like that. I had missed out on those post-pubescent years here in town, so there was a loss. My collegiate friends were in Austin, living their lives. I hadn't told them I was leaving for Omaha and maybe not coming back. I just ghosted; I think I liked it better that way. Well, I thought it was better like that, anyway.

My mom came knocking on my door.

"You didn't go on your run," she said, like it was news to me.

"No, it's cold out."

"It's forty-nine degrees. It's sunny."

"It's freezing."

"Are you more Texan than Nebraskan now?"

"I sent out that mass email. About the transition."

"Oh, it went to my junk folder."

She sat down on my bed and brushed the sides of my face with her mom-soft touch. Smiled at me like it had been a while.

"You know what a junk folder is, Mom?"

"Kind of," she stood and opened the blinds, circulating light into the shadowy room. "I need to get some light in here." I guessed I'd forgotten that I needed light, too.

I could trace back the women in my mom's bloodline six generations. Frances, LouElla, Ursula, Josephine, Kim, Jorah. My grandmother showed me the genealogy work she had done before she died. She sat Mom and me down and opened her giant binder filled with death dates, birth dates, deeds, newspaper articles, last names.

I was named after someone in that book. We all had been. A cousin of my grandmother's who had passed away at a young age. They had been best friends until they were nine years old and she died from some old-timey disease we didn't really have anymore. Josephine talked about this cousin all the time. As if they had a lifetime's worth of memories, not just eight short years. I guessed they were a lifetime's worth if you carried them for that long. Anyway, Mom surprised her, having already decided that, girl or boy, that would be my name. Jorah. You didn't even really know for sure if I was a girl until you got to my middle name. Christine. Because it was popular in the 80s. I owed Jorah forever for saving me from a popular, 80s name.

Our family was impossibly small and verging on extinct. I was the only child, of an only child, of an only child. You could imagine the intrinsic loneliness that came with one person's passing. My grandmother lived with us my whole life until she passed away. She and my mother didn't have one of those tragically cliché mother/daughter relationships. Gossiping and meddling.
They were one. Two roommate best friends. They would have chosen each other even if they could've picked anyone on the planet. That's where I learned the interaction of women. The camaraderie and the support. The honesty and the strength. Right there, in the kitchen I grew up in, coexisted the greatest example of love I'd ever known. Maybe that's why my mom had always been okay without a relationship. Why I was okay without one. Like I said, I preferred to be single, and I assumed after all this time, she did, too.
I knew she missed my grandmother. She'd have taken having her back over a man any day. Why ever ruin perfect, unconditional love with something regular?

"What do you want to do today?" Mom asked me, aimlessly tiptoeing the circumference of my bedroom, maybe checking for dust.

"I don't really have any plans. Why? Did you want to do something?"

She looked at me uncertainly and shrugged her shoulders.

"Only if you're up to it. I'm feeling pretty restless, you know?"

"You are?"

I sat up a little, intrigued.

Restless was my number one emotion.

"Yeah, I don't know."

Her eyes wandered around and then down, thinking.

"I know you're not up for a run, but maybe a walk?" she offered slowly and hopefully. "I'm supposed to be walking anyway, I guess."

"Yes, yeah, I could definitely do that. I can be ready in ten."

"Okay," she turned to leave my room and turned back to me. "I'm really missing Josephine today."

"Okay," I smiled softly at her, understanding that was all either of us needed to say.

Outside, the leaves crunched underneath our sneakers. We walked in a perfect, tandem stride, effortlessly meeting each other's every movement. Our jackets were zipped up past our necks and the bottoms of our lips brushed them when we talked. My ears were chilly and my nose was numb. October weather was as unpredictable as ever. Winter one day. Summer the next. Nebraska often skipped seasons.

"Do you remember when we all used to walk together?" Mom asked me over her zipper. Her shoulders were hunched in to brace herself against the temperature.

"Of course I do. Some of my best times were walking in this neighborhood. This is where you tried to tell me about sex."

"It is?"

"Yeah, you did it out here so you wouldn't have to make eye contact."

"No."

"Yeah, you caved and Josephine had to step in and finish the job."

She shrugged it off; again, not making eye contact.

A group of unidentified birds swirled in the sky above us, zigzagging in a choreographed dance. They were heading to Austin, I decided. In my next few steps, I wished I was a bird. Wings and talons and feathers and free. Our legs pushed on.

"Do you believe in afterlife?" Mom asked me, in an uncomfortable whisper.

"Mom," I shook my head in disbelief. That was probably the last thing I wanted to talk about. Ever.

"I know. I've just been thinking about it a lot today. I'm missing my mother. I wasn't ready to let her go. It doesn't matter how old you are, when you lose your mom it's like you lose your whole compass on life."

I mumbled loud enough to let her know I was listening, but I was actively trying not to listen.

Those conversations were far from my realm of comfort. I would have rather kept things light. At least lighter than thoughts of the afterlife.

"It's not fair to talk to you about this," Mom woke the fuck up. "I'm sorry. I just wanted to hear your opinion."

"I'm sorry you're hurting," I gave her, trying to sound empathetic and not half-assed. I didn't want Mom to hurt, but that was inevitable. I missed Josephine, too. I missed us all together. But I missed a lot of things, and I couldn't get caught up in what I didn't have anymore. I didn't say that, of course. That would consider Josephine just a thing we no longer had -- and that's not what I meant.

Mom and I turned the corner, walking the same path I usually ran. My muscles felt tender and unstretched, so I executed each stride to the fullest. I remembered that the body in rest stays in rest, but it didn't help motivate me. I changed the subject to myself.

"I'm happy to be out of bed, this was a good idea."

"Yes. Me too. I needed to get out of the house and clear my head."

"This is good for your health."

"What about my mental health?"

"Jesus, Mom."

"What?"

"You are never like this."

"I don't get a bad day?"

"I'm just not used to you talking so down."

"Yeah."

"Let's go to the lookout. Maybe that will help."

She hunched her shoulders in and set a more determined pace, with a destination in mind.

"You can look over the town and into the bluffs. I don't know how far you can see today, but we'll be up higher. You need some elevation," I said.

"Is that a medical opinion?"

"It is, indeed."

We finished the last few blocks with silence between us. Conversing with our private thoughts. My mind was trying not to let the morbidity in and focus instead on the stretch of my legs. The familiarity of these streets. Song lyrics. The feeling of my face becoming red. I had been learning to stay in the precious moment and not too far ahead or ever behind. An easier project said than done.

Especially in the surroundings that my past was created from. We trudged up the final incline to the benches and the round cut of concrete they were set in. Mom huffed a little and stood in front of the bench overlooking it all. Her hands on her hips, she breathed in a deep pour of invisible air and exhaled it in a white cloud.

"I can see farther than I thought."

"Yeah, it's pretty clear up here, after all."

"I don't want to be sad," she confessed.

"You don't have to be sad," I said from experience.

"I feel like Mom is still with me."

"Then she is. There is nowhere else she'd rather be."

Mom looked over at me with her face pulled tight and stinging. If her ducts weren't cold, I knew they would have spilled a tear that was welling. But the tears stayed in the rims, clinging to the warm inside.

"I love you," she informed me. I laughed a little bit; I didn't know why.

"I love you too, Mama."

A deep bass started to vibrate the ground around us. I knew they were following their usual route in and out of the roundabout.

"Why on earth do these thugs have that music so loud?"

"Oh. Umm, hold on."

I met the old Buick at the edge of the roundabout, out of Mom's sight. I heard her yelling after me, both nervous and curious, but she stayed put. I guessed she figured no point in both of us getting shot. I ran back to her, and the car finished its loop, the bass still shaking.

"What were you doing?"

"Mom, I need to talk to you about something."

"What did it have to do with that car?"

"Those guys are friends of mine, it's fine. Come sit with me."

Her eyes were wary and alert, but she had a seat next to me. My heartbeat quickened as I opened my hand and revealed the small bag in my palm filled with sticky, green marijuana.

She looked at it and then back up to me.

"What is that?"

"Mom," I said with a hint of caution. "Mom, it's pot."

She recoiled like a cat near water.

"What the hell are you doing? Did you just buy that from them? From drug dealers? What if they were undercover cops? What if you went to jail?"

"Mom, it's all okay. I smoke this sometimes and it makes me feel better."

"Better how?"

"It calms my mind, it heals my body, it unleashes positivity. I didn't want to tell you. But I think it can help you, too."

"You do know that's illegal, right?"

"I do know that it is unfairly regulated and misrepresented, yes. But, it works."

Mom stared through me with the gritty eyes she used when she was disappointed in my choices. A lump in my throat grew heavier as I assumed she was going to kick me out of her house or call the cops to teach me a lesson. I misjudged our closeness; I wrapped my fingers back around the stash and searched for words to backtrack upon, wanting to disappear.

"I'll have some," she said.

"Huh?" my ears deceived me.

"I'll have some, but no one is ever to know."

"Okay..." Before she changed her mind, I pulled my one-hitter out of the most secret pocket of my jacket.

"Oh, look at you, just ready to go."

I ignored this and filled the piece as fast as I could before she changed her mind or chickened out. She didn't watch.

"Do you know how to do this?" I asked.

"I just inhale right?"

"Well, sure. I'll go first."

I bent in to light the pipe and realized I was breaking the law. Not the red-state, fear-mongering, war-on-drugs law but the law of getting high with your parents. The universal law only broken by the few rebels in methed-out, impoverished communities across the nation. Where handing a pipe over was like a rite of passage. I didn't know whether that was fact, but I did know I'd seen some really telling YouTube videos. Yet here we were, me with my mother. My straight-edge mother. On a lookout bench, with a pipe full of street-bought marijuana, about to embark on a journey we both needed, but would never be able to come back from. How did we get here? What would she be like high? Maybe this wasn't a great idea after all. What was I thinking?

"Are we doing this or not? What's up?"

Mom nudged me, with a line between her brows.

"Oh sorry, yes. I mean -- do you want to?"

"Jesus," Mom impatiently took the pipe and lighter from me and tried to light it.

Once. Twice.

I took the lighter gently and lit the end of the piece, we watched the green turn bright orange and then melt together into burnt ash gray.

Mom inhaled in a way that made me think this wasn't her first go at it. Big and deep, her chest puffed out. This was *not* her first time. She exhaled after a long moment. There was no coughing. There was no hacking of instant regret.

There was a calm release of her body as she laid back and turned her head to the sky, eyes wide open. She expertly handed me the pipe and said nothing.

"Mom?"

"Shh. Shh. Let's just sit here."

"Okay," I agreed. I took my own hit, turning my back to my mom to do it. Stooped over it as though she was looking anyway. I met her body language and laid back also, my head looking up at the white and blue sky.

"Look at those birds," Mom pointed to another swirl of black silhouettes flying higher than any birds probably ever had.

"There must be a million up there right now."

"Maybe one of those is Josephine," she said, like she was asking me.

"Mom, I think that is entirely possible."

"She's so high," Mom held out the word until it trailed off with the end of her breath. She raised her arm all the way up. Her fingers pet the birds like precious jewels. Then she laughed. And laughed and laughed and laughed and laughed and laughed and laughed and laughed and laughed and laughed.

# 9

## Walk Through The Alley Of The Shadow Of Death

My friends and I were raised during the swan song of wholesome teenage living. Malls, movies, random Internet, and no cell phones. Stassi did have a pager, of which I was massively jealous. I would page it just to be part of it.

My first AOL account when we got dial-up was *MallQueen4eva*, because after a thousand bored Saturdays the Hot Topic guys at the mall remembered my name, and I was living on a cloud. I would talk to the guys, tossing my hair and never buying anything because I had nothing. You couldn't buy chokers with Bonne Bell. We'd play this game where we fell dramatically in front of people to see if they'd help us up. Easy in platform sandals. We made big deals of it: my falls with arms flailing and cries of "Oh no!"; Stassi more subtle but more sprawled on the ground, Shep bulldozing ahead as if he were a stranger. I didn't know what teenagers did anymore. I didn't think I was supposed to. But the mall shut down. A giant vacancy, filled with our ghosts.

Bowling was what we did when we'd exhausted all our imaginations. Or nights we wanted to get "wild." It was one of those activities where anything could happen. You could have fallen in love if the right song came on, ran into an enemy or teacher. Sneaked a swig of beer if an older table left it. I was the only one to test that. But I never got caught.

This time, it was Shepherd's idea.

To go bowling.

"For old times' sake!"

He was convincing me a few days later, after his massive come clean.

"You know I suck," I said.

"That's why I love playing against you."

"Yeah alright, I'll go."

"I'll see if Stassi's free."

"Just like old times."

"Like I said."

I'd felt a bisection in my life. The things and people that shaped the first half. My mother and grandmother, Shep, Stassi, and the other friends we'd once held dear who had fallen away. And then the things and people who grew me up. With heartbreaks and travels and finding myself. The two combining only within me. How separate those worlds were otherwise. My Austin friends knew every guy I ever dated (post-Shep), every job I walked out of in haste, every bitch I hated and why.

They knew I detested mustard but weren't there the time I discovered I did. They knew Jägerbombs were my drink, not to call me before ten, and they came to all my work events. These guys, Shep and Stassi, knew every embarrassing thing I'd done between the ages of fourteen and eighteen, every lie I told to get out of trouble, every bitch I hated then. But they thought I worked at a kiosk...they didn't care about my adventures, Blue Anise, or Alex. The parts of my life I loved the most. I was still teenage Jorah, doing weird or inappropriate stuff. Early 20s Jorah, drunk and wild. I hadn't grown beyond that to them, I feared. In truth, maybe they hadn't to me, either. Maybe that was the drawback of lifelong friends; you forever saw them in the light you first knew them in. I didn't know what to make of that. I supposed there wasn't anything to make of it at all.

The bowling alley was as I remembered.

Small and dingy. Steeped in late 70s architecture and early 2000s carpet. It smelled like sweat and competition. But, looking around, we were the youngest ones there and they were playing The Who.

"What night is it?"

"Saturday."

"Where are all the teenagers? I wore my spiffy, hipster clothing."

"I don't fucking know, thank god they're not here. They suck."

"Oh," I realized my teenage nostalgia was built for one.

I followed Shepherd up to get our shoes. There was the same woman behind the counter. I remembered her from so many instances of losing my right shoe. She was a hunchbacked, sturdy thing, with gray hair that was just turning when I knew her, and a crooked nose.

"Hi!" I said cheerfully, like I may have said back then.

"What size?"

"Nine! I have big feet for a little girl," I said, hoping she would have remembered the times she had said that to me. If she didn't, I sounded like a huge dork. She just ducked behind to find the shoe, and I slammed my ballet flats onto the counter.

"How does she not remember me?" I asked Shepherd, angrier than I thought.

"Why would she?"

"We used to come here all the time. I was her favorite."

"We came here like ten times."

"No way. No fucking way!"I screamed at the top of my lungs and watched Shepherd take a step back from me.

The woman threw her head up from behind the counter.

"Hey, hey! Not that kind of language in here, missy!" she scolded, and I could have sworn we'd been here and done that before.

"Why don't you remember me?" I pointed to myself, pleading with her. "It's me. I used to come here with him. Seventeen years ago. Forever ago? I know you see a lot of kids, but remember me? I was the big-foot, little girl. And I used to say 'I'm not that little' because I was an asshole kid. And I didn't realize that was actually a very sweet and endearing thing for you to do. You remembered me like that...and now you don't. Now you can't." I stood on my toes to look her square in the eye. What was I doing? Shepherd stood behind me silent and transfixed, not knowing what to say.

I rubbed my arm, my head down. What the hell was my problem?

"How many games do you want?" she continued.

"Umm," I looked over at Shepherd to make sure we were even staying.

"Let's just do one for now," he said quietly.

"Just one...for now."

She took my one shoe and handed me two.

"I'm going to kick your ass," I tied into my red and blue shoes, trying to ignore that Shepherd hadn't spoken.

I dropped my head and heaved an audible, yet not attention-seeking, sigh.

"I'm sorry," I told him. Apologies had never come hard for me, especially when they were earned.

"I don't know what came over me," I half lied.

"I've, like, never seen anyone act like that." He said that like a traumatized child who just had his first brush with it. "I feel bad for that woman."

"Did you see her? It didn't even phase her," I argued. "I've apologized -- I mean it. Can we just move on?"

"Yeah. Can I take a few minutes to get over it? Jeez."

"Yeah, take your time."

Feel bad for all the people you were ripping off at work, Shep.

Where was Stassi?

My plan would be just as immature as it had always been. I'd corner Stassi, admit to what I'd done before Shepherd could tell her his version, and then we'd gang up on him to get over it. Girl 102. Advanced move.

"Hey, hey, hey," like clockwork, Stassi danced over in full-on knitwear with a pitcher of light beer.

"Hey," I said in surprise. "You look ready to party."

"Babysitting husband and no curfew. Oh, yes. Hey, Shep."

"Hey," he muttered.

"What's wrong with him?"

"He doesn't like the way I act," I said.

"Shut up, Shep," she came to my aid. "The night isn't even started yet."

"Thanks, Stass."

"Don't be a wet fart," she added, pouring beers. Stassi and I cracked up as Shep faced the inevitable: having to move on. He put our names in the machine.

Asshole.

Douchey.

Shep.

Picked up his ball and sent it down the lane. Stassi turned to me.

"I'll be Asshole."

"Douchey is my middle name," I retorted.

"I haven't been here in years," she said, looking around. "I mean -- there's no time for bowling anymore."

"They have those kiddie-bowling helping things," I let her know.

"I'm not bringing my kids in this germ trap! There's probably

HIV everywhere in here," she took a swig of her beer, her lips to the glass.

"You guys aren't even going to watch me?" Shep lurched over, with a disappointed look.

"We're catching up. Relax, Shep!"

"Here," Stassi poured and handed him a beer; he looked at it skeptically.

"You didn't get any limes with this?" he asked.

"I'm up next," Asshole jumped to her feet and lined up her shot, leaving Shep staring at the cold glass.

"I gotta go find some limes," he took off to the bar.

Stassi rolled her first ball. Eight pins.

"Yup," she put her arms up and turned with flair. Classic. I clapped for her, as was customary, and finished my beer. She went again, the ball flowing smoothly between two pins.

"Your turn, Douchey," she chided. "Where's Shep?"

"On the great lime search."

She rolled her eyes.

"You really want a lime in this place? Probably crawling with Listeria," she lifted her glass to her lips again, and I laughed to myself. I took my turn with a lime green eight-pounder. Five pins on the first bowl and gutter on the second. About as good as ever.

"So," Stassi leaned in with this mischievous face upon my return.

"So?"

"You and Shep."

"Nope."

"You guys belong together. Look at him, all grumpy because of the limes and you're like 'Look at him, so grumpy,'" she made herself laugh.

"Are you drunk?"

"Happens fast," she burped.

"Oh, okay," I giggled. "No, Shep and I, we are just friends. I feel like I have this conversation with you every time I'm in town."

"We do."

"Okay."

Shep bumbled down to us with a defeated look on his face.

"They're out of limes," he cried out.

"Do they have lime juice?"

"It's not the same. Oh well," he begrudgingly poured himself a second fill. I couldn't help but wonder how many other little things affected him so negatively. I must've really upset him.

"He's always like this," Stassi read my mind. "He comes over for dinners every Sunday, and I have to make sure I have limes for his Bud Lights."

"You guys see each other every week?"

"Mm-hm," she nodded.

I wondered what the hell my life would be like if I saw those two every week. What would we talk about? I was on the outside and, although I'd known that for years, it felt -- icky. I wanted to infiltrate, to be initiated again.

"I don't think I have anything going on this Sunday," I offered, to invite myself.

"Oh, it's kind of a thing we just do," she motioned to her and Shep, who had just botched his turn and was heading back. He switched places with Stassi.

"I'm rusty as hell," he confided.

"That's probably a good thing. Who needs to be bowling enough to be good at it?"

"It's an Olympic sport."

"I don't know that that's true," I logged it in my mind to Google. "So you and Stassi have dinner every Sunday? That's nice."

"Yeah, and her husband and kids and random selections of his friends."

"Oh. So it's not just you guys?"

"Uh-uh. You should come one night."

I was not going to do that shit. I mean, I would have hated Sunday dinner but that didn't mean I shouldn't have been invited. Just like the bar. Why wouldn't Stassi want me to come and hang out? Don't take it personally. I reminded myself of one of my many mantras over the years. Don't take it personally. It was about her, not you.

It was my turn to bowl, and I was already over it. I didn't care about that germ-ridden, heavy-ass ball rolling down that oily-ass lane to hit those stupid-ass pins. I didn't care about stupid meals at Stassi's stupid house or Shep's dumb limes. That was exactly what got me out of there in the first place so long ago. It all came back to me like a bowling ball to the skull. I'd made a major mistake. What did I think was going to happen? I'd come back home and everything was colored just for me? How ridiculous. How selfish. I dropped my second ball down the pine with absolutely zero effort and turned back to hit the bar.

"You're not going to watch me?" Shep called.

"No!"

I shook my head and beelined for strangers, real strangers -- not known ones. I sat at the bar; it was sticky, and the selection behind it was unusual. A mix of schnapps and flavored liqueurs. Creme De Menthe, anyone?

"What can I get you?" the bartender looked like the woman from the front of house. Identical. I looked over, but she was still there.

"My sister," she answered without being asked. "We look like twins, but I'm younger. But you knew that."

"Do you remember me?" I leaned in and showed her my face.

"From what, baby?"

"From here. Did you ever do the shoes?"

"Yeah, sure did."

"So, years ago, almost twenty years ago...I would come here and you or she would always say, 'Size nine. Big feet for --'"

"For a little girl. Yeah, I used to say that. It was you and one other, and you two had the biggest feet of the girls that came in here. Wow, that was fourteen lifetimes ago. Don't tell me you've been sitting around thinking about that shit since then."

I laughed out loud. "No, no way. I just wanted to know if you remembered it."

"I remember it but I haven't been thinking about it, either."

"That's okay."

"Why don't I make you one of my specialties? My version of a Mind Eraser."

"Oh, that sounds glorious."

"You're not driving are you?"

"No, ma'am."

She started to mix the oddest collection of alcohol into a silver mixer; she added some milk, and I didn't want to know the expiration date. That was where I felt at home, sitting at a bar, talking to a stranger and finding that common bond. A cocktail, a laugh.

"Sometimes you just need somebody to tell you you're not crazy," she said, over the final pour.

She handed me the drink; I pushed all doubts out of my mind and ingested. It was cold and unbelievably strong and delicious. I sucked it down fast.

"Easy, it's a panty dropper."

I took the advice and answered her previous question.

"Yeah, sometimes I just like to know that someone remembers the experience of me, as I do of them. Like, I'm not making this up."

"Yup, yup. I get that."

I smiled at her, happy I gave myself the opportunity to break out and have a new conversation.

"Like those illegals coming up here, now I'm not alone in the fact that makes me uncomfortable, but I'm the only one to say it."

Um.

"Or this wackadoodle idea that black lives matter more than mine. Am I crazy? If it wasn't for white people, would they even be in this great country? Where's the gratefulness? I had to bring this up at church last week --"

Oh my good god.

"I think it's my turn to bowl," I stood up from the bar to head back to the game. What the fuck was happening?

"Oh honey, that'll be eight bucks."

I played through my games on autopilot.

My mind was a thousand other places. But also very, very much there.

Stassi and Shepherd were closer than Shepherd and I. When did that happen? Shepherd was always mine. My firsts. I supposed it was my doing. I moved, I pushed, I trivialized.

God, they were so blah.

Separate they were fun. Together? Shep was needy, and Stassi was shady. Two on one.

They just repeated other people's jokes and then laughed at each other; I watched them with squint eyes. Such *boredom*. Such blah.

I mean, the bitch at the bar was crazy but she was living out loud.

She was Whaaaa?

If they were Blah and she was Whaaaa?

What did that make me?

I was a total Blam. Shaka Laka.

I was Blam Shakalaka.

The math and sciences of people, man.

They were a better match for each other. I was other. I was Blam. Shaka. Laka.

I.Was.
drUNk.
It took nothing those days. A bigot and a cocktail, and I was under.
I was a shitty bowler.
I was scared.
I was running.
I was more than Omaha.
I was special.
Hahahahahahahahaha.
I was laughing at myself.
I was no one.
I was a dead woman walking.
I was dirt.
I was --

"You're turn, slacker!"

Up.
I was up.
It was "your" not "you're," you fucking idiot.
Shepherd.
I shook the thoughts out of my tired mind and tried to knock at least one pin down.
Just one damn pin.
The room was spinning, and the ball was heavier than it should have been. Heavier than it ever was.
I saw Stassi, and I wanted inside her head. Everything was guarded and devised.
I saw Shepherd at the scoreboard, waiting impatiently, wanting to get home to his limes. Wanting to win. They both wanted to win at something, but I didn't know what. Or who else was playing. I knew that I wasn't.
I was a mean person.
I was better than this stupid bowling alley.
I was hungry.

My legs wobbled underneath me, and I stepped up the two inches to the lane. There was a guy next to me following proper etiquette and waiting for me to go. I waved him on. He walked up to his lane, and I watched him like a hawk. I went up to his lane and threw my ball right before he could and I laughed and laughed and laughed in his face. The room spun more and more. It was so fast I couldn't keep up with it. I felt the familiar lunge of my guts heave underneath my ribcage.

I was puking.

I didn't know where Shepherd was.

I didn't know where Alex was.

He wasn't there.

I left him there.

I didn't know who was helping me.

I didn't know what Stassi thought.

I just saw black.

Stupid disco ball.

Black.

Faces.

Disco ball.

Lights.

Black.

Black.

Black.

# 10

## The Thing

The tumor was three inches in and three-and-a-half back on the left side. It had tentacles, like an unforgiving and homicidal octopus that had crawled through the crevices of my brain and attached. Rendering me inoperable. I imagined the streets and avenues of my brain being filled with this odious, green serpent-servant of destruction turning out light after light.

The memory of something that happened sometime when I was five. How to do long math. The sound of my grandmother's voice. Until there were only the final basics left: how to breathe, how to eat, where to shit. And maybe those wouldn't last either.

The only people that knew were my mother and Alex.

Alex, who had been taking care of me for the last year. Who was using every dime of our extra money for treatment, for comfort food, for trials.

I gave up chemo two months ago and hadn't felt so good in a long time. But what was coming was inevitable. That was why we couldn't talk. We didn't know what to say. I didn't have space in me to comfort him. And that was what it turned into.

"You're going to be fine. Look, you get the remote control all the time," I would laugh, giving levity to the human fear of facing mortality. My own mortality, and I was supposed to be light about it, because the worst thing you could do was pass that fear on to the ones you loved. The living.

We both knew what I came here for. So we just left it in Texas, behind us. Sweet, juicy, messy, loving memories.

When I decided to cease treatments, when it became about quality over quantity, I wanted to come home.

I had this romantic notion in my head of what home meant. I saw everything as different than I actually knew it to be. Slower, prettier. There was a wraparound porch and fresh-squeezed juice. Friendships that felt like down coats in the winter and ice cubes in the summer. Old neighbors that asked about every member of your family and remembered when you were just this tall -- and they motioned at their knees. Home had somehow become this Margaret Mitchell southern fantasyland in my fevered, hopeful mind, instead of the reality. There was no wraparound porch, just a spot of concrete and a few potted plants. There was no fresh-squeezed anything. My friendships were wet blankets on windy nights. The neighbors didn't talk to each other. There was barely any family.

I realized that all too late. Wheels-bouncing-down-on-the-tarmac-of-Eppley too late.

Coming home was supposed to fulfill my circle of life. Wasn't that the rule, the hero returned to his hometown carrying the head of the giant he'd slain and preaching all the wisdom he learned on his long journey? I thought that when I stepped foot back onto hometown soil, something magical would manifest, and I would be made whole and ready for the next step of my great, parting sorrow.

"I don't think you should do this. Omaha doesn't make you happy. You have never been happy going back there," Alex warned me. Even my mom, who had tried to convince me to come back nearly every day since I had left, changed her tune.

"Are you sure you want to do this? I mean, I could always come to Austin. There's so much more sun there. You love the sun." But I was bound and determined to come home and complete my saga.

"You may not understand, but I have to do this," I remembered telling them both -- very seriously, sounding like I needed a cape and a mask more than a hospital gown and final arrangements.

They were appalled at the cessation, of course. After all that *we'd* been through. After all the needles poked through *our* skulls and blood drawn from *our* arms. Days and days of nausea and shaking, seizures, migraines, mostly side effects of medicine. Trials and experiments and desperation for anything that made it better. I was supposed to be stronger and continue to push through, so the three of us could join hands at the end and run a marathon in my honor or something. But I was tired. And the medicines were the worst part of everything.

Alex would carry me some nights to the shower and back to bed, my legs too weak to stand under my slight weight. He patted my head with cool washcloths and asked my doctors all the questions I'd forgotten.

He'd work extra to cover things our insurance didn't. And one, very memorable time, he wiped my ass. He was a prodigious caretaker. I could feel his love all the way down to my toenails. I would hear him on the phone with my mother in the next room, discussing what should be done and the next best move.

I was consuming their lives. I was taking them with me, and *that* made me sick.

I felt weaker and worse with every new pill I put into my fading body. I made the decision then. Full stop. I would much rather die me, than a bone-bodied guinea pig. Without the medications, sometimes I forgot I was sick at all. So it was all worth it.

Worth took on a new meaning at that time.

Mom refinanced her house. She flew us all over the country. And she hated to fly. She courted conversations with top surgeons, stayed up late researching. Because it was worth it, to her. Any cost, any flight -- my life was her cause, and it was all so worth it. It wasn't to me. And that was hard for her to understand. It wrenched a steely, deep twist in the bottom of my gut, her hope did. I knew it stemmed from the strange cocktail of love, fear, and hate that cancer shook up and poured. It held your mouth open and made you swallow it, no matter how vigorously you shook your head no.

Cancer gave zero fucks.

My mom was so scared that if she didn't find and utilize hope she'd bury herself right next to me. I wasn't supposed to leave her first. It was just the two of us. A dangerous family math, in and of itself.

She was supposed to leave me, decades into the future. Like *Grey Gardens* if I never got married. Two aging spinsters that cooked each other dinner, dressed alike, and made each other mad.

If by a miracle of the universe I happened to find some version of domestic existence and started a family with some poor sap, Mom would have a room in our home -- the east side of the home -- and die surrounded by me and my grieving children, knowing that her only child was safe and loved, and that there would be legacy.

More than anything, way more than my own looming mortality, I cared only about what this would do to her. A life before and after her only child. And me, just a brief fleeting person she used to know. That was the hardest pill to swallow.

She hadn't dated a man in years. First, because she didn't want to disrupt my childhood with the cigarette-smoking, tank-top-wearing, loser Joes she usually liked. Men like my father, so I heard.

And later, because she was a strong, independent black woman who didn't need no man. That had left me happy for her and also scared. Who would she lean on? Where would she go?

"I don't want you to worry about me," she whispered over me one night as I fell asleep after a bad episode in Utah, where we often went for experimental treatment.

I was writhing in an uncontrollable cold, feverish pain. My head throbbing so loudly, thumping in my ears. I would have welcomed death that night.

"I'll find you," she whispered, ready to let me go. Ready to see me at peace.

She said that, and I logged the tears that fell from her eyes onto my face in my permanent memory. The memory that I wouldn't let any cancerous aggression steal from me. I would hold on to those even through whatever transition death was; I would hold them with me until everything everywhere ceased to exist.

"I'll find you, too," I said in the back of my mind. "Mama, I'll find you, too."

We were not brought together in the flesh of this earth only to be permanently severed by something as natural as death. I would have found her, no matter where I landed.

I swore it.

# 11

## You Can Run...

I HID OUT FOR DAYS AFTER THE BOWLING ALLEY.

I was unresponsive, unconscious that night. They called an ambulance and turned me to my side while I vomited and shook. Stassi rode with me, carrying my purse and jacket; I remembered her stroking my hair. Shepherd called my mom and told her what happened -- that I had drank too much and I probably hadn't eaten. She ran to the hospital to meet me there. When she burst through the door she was in pajama pants, curlers, and an old coat, with bits of green mask around the edges of her face. They dripped an IV into my arm and asked me about my medical history.

I didn't say anything about anything. They could figure it out.

"She drank a LOT of vodka," Stassi filled everyone in.

"What are you doing?" Mom panicked. "You are not supposed to be drinking." She pulled back from the kisses she'd been giving me. My face went cold and guilty.

"I am -- fine, Mom. Let's be alone."

Mom flipped around and acknowledged Stassi for the first time. She pulled her in for a hug.

"Hi, sweetheart, thank you. Thank you so much."

"No problem, I'm just so glad she's okay."

"I'm okay. Thank you for coming with me."

"Of course."

"Shepherd is still in the waiting room," Mom told her. "Why don't you guys get home?"

"Okay, I'll call you tomorrow." She took my hand and gave me a pitiful look. There was no doubt this story would make the rounds.

"Goodnight."

Mom put her head down, her curlers bounced off her heaving shoulders.

"Mommy."

"I can't do this, baby. I thought this was it. I thought this was it."

I sat up and hugged her as much as my IV drip allowed. My head still throbbed through the morphine. The pain was gone, but the dull tension remained.

"I'm sorry. I only had a couple drinks. I don't know what happened."

"Running here, not knowing if I was going to be able to see you, to talk to you. I thought this was it."

She looked at me with a trembling lip and a dented brow. She looked at me with stretch marks, and breast feeding, and first steps and the first day of school, and first period and first boyfriend, and watching me sleep and checking me for breath...

"I'm sorry, Mom."

That's all I could say through the repulsion I felt for myself.

I avoided everyone for three days after that.

Isn't that when Jesus rose?

After three days in the tomb.

If the Lord himself could take three days to lay low and chill, then I certainly could.

My phone had been blowing up with calls and texts, so I turned it off. My mom let everyone know I was okay and back at home, resting. I didn't tell Alex. I wanted to, I wanted to use it as a guilt trip, a reason he should be here by my side. In the end, that's why I was quiet about it. Sometimes the things that guilted you the most were the things you didn't know about.

We were hiding out, the both of us.

I barely left my bedroom in those days. My head was still swimming from all the chemicals, natural and not. My eyes sensitive to light. Myself, embarrassed. Nothing was mild anymore. It was scary and fucked or it was not happening. My mother hovered over me, like a paid nurse, but she kissed my eyes and prayed in tongues; her face was long with fear and eyes red-rimmed. When she knew I was awake and safe, she'd exit the room quickly, leaving me be. I could barely speak to her, hating what I'd put her through. Hating that it wasn't the last time or the worst time she'd cry over me. If it weren't for this body, I could live forever.

On the fourth morning, I felt as though the cloud cover had lifted. My head was lighter, my emotions subsiding. I gave Mom my blessing to leave the house, that I'd be fine alone. Reluctantly, she did. I checked in with myself to see what kind of energy I had. There was nothing there. Cognizant though bedridden, there were worse states to be in. I reached my hands down to the side of the bed and felt for the smooth edges of my laptop. Maybe I could look at the screen without a lightning bolt going through my brain. While the screen was still blue, I turned the brightness to the dimmest setting. It was okay.

Through all this excitement, I missed Alex's first shoot without me. His first shoot with our intern, Paul. I was sure it went off without a hitch. I was sure it was wonderful, but also I hoped it fell spectacularly to pieces. I hoped Paul choked. I hoped Alex broke down on set and couldn't continue and that the client would demand a refund unless I came back and fixed it all myself. I would have jumped on the plane and put out the fire and everyone would say:

"What would we do without her?"

Those clients came to us after seeing our work in *Wedding Day*. They planned their date around our future availability. Almost a year ago. We were all so confident a year ago, it blew my fucking mind. She cried when we told her I wouldn't be on hand to shoot their wedding anymore. But we eased their fears -- the best we could. Like two loving parents breaking divorce news to the kids. With soft voices and our hands on their knees. And a twenty percent discount.

I wondered, in a sad part of me, if I would have been able to shoot. I brought my camera; it was here, packed away. I hadn't lifted it at all. Treatments had made me frail and sick. The camera weighted me down like a stone. I'd gotten dizzy standing for long periods of time. I'd have puked if I pushed myself. I had all these warrior mantras in my head, written on my walls, on my palms. Those only served to make me feel like a failure when I was weakened beyond my ability to "rise above." All that changed in the first weeks of stopping treatment. I wasn't frail anymore. I gained a small amount of weight back. I got to look normal until the end. Very deceptive. I could run, I could eat. But I had yet to pick up my camera again. Small, finessed movements worked against my brain's capabilities, and I was scared to fail a shutter click. The circular movement of finding the right speed. Of replacing a lens cap. The precious second-nature things I was the most scared to lose.

I pulled the client file from the back end of our website with baited breath.

Relief and disdain. No one choked; of course, they didn't. You did not choke after ten years with a reputation like Blue Anise. I gave in with a smile. They were gorgeous: bright, but surprising. He used some of the shots that I mapped out, with my go-to filters. He didn't forget me.

"Alex, you bitch," I murmured, jealously satisfied.

I reached for my phone and turned it on, ignoring the deluge of incoming messages.

I moved to text Alex, again wondering about my fingers.

They glided effortlessly and expertly over the buttons. I wasn't thinking about my fingers, wasn't thinking about my fingers, I wasn't thinking about my -- fuck. Typo.

*You're a genius. These are perfect.*

I hoped to see his text bubbles come up immediately, but they didn't. So I waited. I flipped over to his Facebook. He hadn't posted in days.

That was good. He was busy and thinking about work.

That was bad. He never let a day go without sharing something. Usually a piece of bad poetry or a prank video. The extremes.

I slowly dialed his number. I was still really good about remembering people's phone numbers. A rare talent and a force of old habit.

It rang once and my throat filled. Twice and my stomach dropped. Three times and I almost hung up. Four times and he answered.

"Hey," he croaked.

"Hi."

There was a rustling on his end, and I waited for him to talk next.

"How are you?"

"I'm okay. I'm good," I said. It was all relative: how accurate that statement was.

"Your mom told me what happened."

"Oh. I didn't know that."

"When I didn't hear from you I called her."

"It's okay. I'm just really coming back to life right now."

"You sound good."

"The pictures look perfect. How was the shoot? How was Paul?"

"Paul was an expert. He'll be great on our team. I'm so happy you like them, I was thinking of you the whole time. What would Jorah do?"

"You used my shots!"

"They're what landed the job. Paul shot most of those."

My ego twisted.

"Oh. Did he."

"Don't be mad; it's still your baby. You were missed."

"Good." I took a breath and then asked, "When are you coming up?"

His response was quick, "I don't know."

"Alex! You said! You said one week, two max."

"We're so busy down here, you know."

"Well, you have Paul now, so he can save the day," I spat petulance.

"You know it doesn't work like that. I will come to you."

"What if -- what if the other night was it? You don't know!"

There was a cumbersome silence, filled with questions and hypotheticals.

After a while:

"How are your other friends?"

"Boring."

"Jorah."

"They're not you, I need you. I don't need you," I corrected myself. "I want you."

"I'll be there soon."

"I miss you."

"I miss you," he said after a lifetime.

# 12

## Advice From Stepford

You know, we can't drink like we used to. After thirty, your risk for stroke goes up, and drinking increases your risk for breast cancer. I bet you were just dehydrated and seriously, all the sugar in those crappy shots. Your body just processes them like you're drinking syrup. And that shows up on your face. That's why I really don't drink. That and the kids. I swear, if the twenty-four-year-old Stassi could see me now, she'd be pouring booze down my throat. I never drank as much as you. And that was for the best, I saw where it took you. But seriously, health at our age is of the utmost importance because NOW we have to avoid aging! And alcohol leads to aging and wrinkles and all that stuff. I was scared. I was scared for you. One second, you're up drinking and dancing and the next second, you're down. Your eyes were literally rolling in the back of your head, and you were shaking. I instantly went into mom mode and cradled your head. Do you remember that? And I yelled at someone, anyone to call 911. Do you remember that? I've never seen someone have a seizure: god, it was scary. I was so worried for you. I thought, 'I cannot let my best friend DIE in a bowling alley like this.' But, the paramedics came and said we did the right thing, and I jumped in the ambulance because that's the kind of person I am. Well, anyway, I'm just glad you're okay, and I hope you learned something from this. But, side-note, you should look at some of my anti-aging products. Just a few fingertips a night can take YEARS off your life. Or, I mean, the life of your face. You can look so much younger. We HAVE to start now. I'm not kidding. And -- the other thing, and I don't think you should take this the wrong way, but you know I'm going to SpiritCycle, and I think you should come with me. I think you're doing some soul-searching now -- I mean, there's no other explanation for a slip-up like that. So, you should come with me and give it a shot. I know, I know -- this is so not like anything I ever thought I'd be doing, but it's fun. I mean, I'm getting stuff out of it. I'm like -- what if there is an all-powerful universe or God or something? What if I DID look good as a brunette now? What if Target was purple instead of red, would it still be popular? You know? I just come up with all this stuff I'd never thought of before. Aaron and I are even going to take a date night. I mean, I initiated it. We never leave our house! Together, anyway. So, maybe you would like it. You can come with me this Wednesday. I'll come pick you up. Well, call me when you get this! Byeeee."

# 13

## My History with Stassi

When I was a teenager, I thought I was going to be a writer. I'd write long-winded and melancholy verses and publish them to nowhere under my pen name.

Verona.

That was the me before Shep. Before learning that the wiles of teenage passion were more pizza parlors than *Wuthering Heights*. But, I thought we all had that phase, maybe? Where everything hurt. And everyone was a sellout. And no one got us.

And blue eye shadow and feathered headbands. And Delia's catalogs. And Fastball.

I'd stay up late and watch Conan O'Brien and Greg Kinnear -- back when he was a talk-show host -- feeling cultured. I'd flip through magazines, circling product, feeling cosmopolitan. I'd sleep on the floor with the windows open on summer nights and cover my bedroom walls with pastel painted nudes, feeling like Gwyneth Paltrow in *Great Expectations.*

I thought I was so original.

I was just copying things people did in movies. Gluing quarters to the floor and all that. Wearing black lipstick and all that.
The only teenager that ever lived.

When I met Stassi, she was reading an *Animorphs* book, wearing pigtails, and talking shit about boy bands. She was laying in a hammock at a mutual friend's house, swinging back and forth and just a few months older than myself.

Stassi and I couldn't have been more different, but we clicked. She had friends who could drive and was obsessed with *Buffy the Vampire Slayer*. I was a lit nerd with a wild side; it was a natural mix. There were beers in her parents' basement that we never drank, books we shared, and those long, drawn-out conversations that started at prime time and lasted past midnight. I talked about how I wanted to be a writer. A poet, of course: traveling the world while writing personalized poems. She wanted to be an actress. And a mom. And we'd each tell the other that we'd be great at what we wanted to do, and we'd cheer us on forever.
Somewhere, and sooner than I expected, that cheering came to a halt.

*You've Got Mail* had just come out, and I was obsessed. I zeroed in on the typewriters. I thought, "That's what I need if I'm going to be a professional poet." Convinced "professional poet" was an actual career. Ah, the optimism of the 90s.
I passionately confessed this to Stassi. I scoured through pictures of old models and stumbled upon a baby-blue Smith Corona inside a matching carrying case. It stole my heart.
We had a typewriter at my house, a relic from my mother's childhood. But, I just had to have this one.

"Why do you want a typewriter? Just write it on a computer. That is so outdated," Stassi warned me.

"No, it's romantic. The sound, the paper, the urgency of picking the right word."

"Okayyy."

"Just support me on this quest and know that when I become famous and make a million dollars, I'll take care of you."

"I'll let you know if I see any typewriters lying around."

She said that with disbelief and rolled eyes, but she did help me look for one. She combed thrift stores and newspapers and the new site eBay. She asked her mom's friends -- I felt it was just as important to her that I found this perfect tool as it was to me. Although, it was seeming more and more that my dream typewriter no longer existed. I was almost ready to settle for the normal, run-of-the-mill, black or gray ones.

Until one day I got a phone call at home, and it was Stassi. It was an early Saturday morning. I remember Saturday mornings as a kid because they all felt the same. Mom was always gone, and I'd watch One Saturday Morning on ABC with a bowl of cereal, feeling independent.

"Guess. What I have!!" Stassi's sing-song voice came through the receiver clear and crisp.

"Oh my god! What?"

"A beautiful, excellent condition blue typewriter WITH a case."

I nearly dropped the bowl out of my shaking hands.

"You do?? Really? Oh my god!!"

I was jumping up and down with tears in my eyes and milk sloshing down my arm.

"I'm going to be a writer! I'm going to be a writer!" I started screaming.

It took a second before I realized that I was screaming alone.

"Stass? Are you there? Can you come over? When can I get it? How much was it?"

She cleared her throat a little.

"Well, actually, this one is for me."

"What do you mean: 'this one'?"

"Like, I really love it. And my mom found it because she knew I'd been looking for one. So, I'm going to keep this one."

"But, you were looking for one for me."

"I know."

"Are you being serious? You know how bad I've wanted this. We've been looking everywhere."

"No, I know. And we WILL find you one. It's just not this one. I think, through all of your excitement I just ended up wanting one, too. I mean, my mom got this. It's like a gift. I can't just hand it over to you, you know. We'll keep looking. I gotta go. Bye!"
She hung up the phone in my ear and the line cut. I slowly dropped the receiver to my side and tried to process everything I was feeling in that split second. I wasn't exactly understanding how me wanting a blue typewriter had transmuted into Stassi having one. Did she expect me to be happy for her? Because it sounded like she wanted me to be happy for her. I sank slowly back into my seat, sugary pink milk still coating my skin, and lost -- just a little bit of my innocence.

That may have been where it started to go south with Stassi, but it was the very tippy top of the iceberg of the Antarctica that was our friendship. There were a few weeks of the silent treatment and Stassi passively-aggressively asking me what was wrong, with the typewriter tucked under her arm like a stack of books. She carried it around with her in the halls like a prize jewel, and I heard the other kids go up to her with "oohs" and "ahhs," wondering where she got it, and what it was, and how original. I wanted to slam my locker closed with her in it. I hadn't written anything in weeks, and I blamed her. Even then, I was aghast at her lack of self-awareness. I knew that as teenagers we were supposed to be selfish and dumb, but I thought that as friends we weren't.

But, her need for attention faded, as did her interest in the typewriter, as did my anger. And sooner rather than later, we were best friends again. Although I would always be more cautious with the things I shared. Stassi continued to take on parts of me for herself; the things that set us apart became less polar. But nothing stuck like that first time.

Years later, after I'd moved away, I took notice of Stassi's new friends and how much she drew from them. The same haircut here. Exact same glasses there. Opinions that shifted from her parents' ideals to those of whoever she was dating. I wondered if anyone noticed or if it was just me. Did she even notice? I wondered if she would ever have a chance to be herself, free from the influence of everyone around her, even if it meant losing control. Even if it meant doing something scary. They said imitation was the sincerest form of flattery; I said it's the clearest form of insecurity. And insecure people scared the living shit out of me.

When Stassi was pregnant with her first baby, I came home for two weeks. I'd never spent much time around a pregnant person and was curious, although I also wanted to show my support. It was the summer we turned thirty.

"Do you have any names picked out yet?"

"Oh, we've gone over so many and just can't agree on anything. Penelope. We both like that."

"Very cute! I love that name," I said, genuinely excited.

"I do, too...so, maybe that's it. There are just so many names to choose from, it's overwhelming."

"I'm sure the right one will pop up. Right? I mean, every baby needs a name," I was shaky in my confidence. There was something about being around her, and that gigantic baby-filled stomach, that set me on edge. In a softer way. I watched my language more; I found myself whispering and saying sentences too saccharine to be mine.

"If you ever had a baby what would you name her?"

"I have thought about this SO much."

"Really?" Stassi turned her nose up like the whole idea smelled like ass.

"Yes, really. Just in case. There's always a just-in-case. Ever since I was eight I've thought if I had a girl, I'd name her Josephine."

"After your grandma. I remember you saying that now."

"Yeah," I beamed with this small secret I'd only ever shared with her.

"I mean, who knows, I may change my mind one day. I'm not hardcore 'no kids.' I just will NOT be missing my pill anytime soon."

"I can't even see you with kids. Won't you miss the nightlife?"

"Stassi, what are you talking about? All I do is work. The nightlife?" I laughed at her willful blurring of my life's timelines. "Blue Anise IS my kid right now. I'm just saying, I'm open to anything."

"Oh. Well, Josephine is a nice name," she offered.

"I think my grandmother would love to pass it on to the next generation. So we'll see!"

After three days, Stassi was in labor. Fourteen hours and a C-section later, she called me to come meet her little one. I swooped in and picked up this tiny, pink bundle into my arms.

"I've never held anything so small," I smiled, feeling so proud of what Stassi had created. She was going to be amazing.

"What'd you name her?" I asked, staring down onto her mile-long eyelashes and flushed skin.

"Josephine."

# 14

## Triple Feature

Shepherd asked me if I wanted to see a triple feature. I was certain after the bowling alley, he wouldn't be wanting to see me again. But he'd moved on. I guessed me being rushed to the hospital bought me points.

I asked myself if I had the patience. If I died tomorrow, would I want my last day on earth spent shuffling from film to film, eating hard popcorn, and making snide remarks as people sidestepped us to get to the bathroom?

I didn't remember the last time I saw a movie in a theater.

Definitely before there were any shootings in them.

Now, they all sounded terrible.

People eating and drinking cocktails -- chairs vibrating. If you wanted an at-home experience, go home. You could fart at home. There were blankets there.

I didn't need to watch a movie with a roomful of strangers, all wishing we were slightly more comfortable, and smelling each other's dinner entrées.

I'd been bringing my own food into movie theaters for years. I could have made a killing.

"We'll probably be the only ones there," he said.

"I'll go," I said.

Shepherd chose the movies, like he liked to do.

That was to be my redemption for the bowling alley, and I hoped he accepted it.

"We have a comedy, a drama, and a thriller today. We're hitting it all."

"Okay!"

He had just picked me up and his car smelled like his cologne. He always wore the same scent: Cool Water. They said that scent was the strongest tie to memory, and I was seventeen again with that smell.

Shepherd was shaven nicely, wearing his signature plaid button-up over a t-shirt, with a beanie. He was eighteen and adorably excited.

"I don't want to tell you what we're seeing. I'd rather you be surprised."

"Alright. But there are things I hate."

"You'll be fine."

"You'll be fine" was our universally-used shortcut for "Your feelings don't really matter, please stop bitching and enjoy the ride."

I buckled my seatbelt and shut the hell up.

"Do you want to talk about what happened?" Shepherd asked me, chewing on his bottom lip.

"Not really," I looked at him and then out my window. "I mean, do you?"

"No. Well, yes, I mean. Are you alright? I've never seen

someone go to the hospital for drinking. I thought that was all you did down in Texas."

"That was a long time ago."

Jesus...did no one follow my Instagram?

"So then, what is it? The altitude?"

I shook my head.

"We're at sea level, Shepherd."

"Well, we have the bluffs! And Texas is going to fall in the ocean, so..."

"No...it's nothing like that. I wasn't feeling well that night; I wasn't feeling myself. I shouldn't have been drinking, but I didn't have that much."

"Yeah. And that whole flipping out thing."

"Yeah, that."

"I was scared. I was, like, scared for you."

Had he and Stassi practiced their twin remarks?

"You shouldn't be. I was fine. Mom said you guys waited in the waiting room for a while. Thank you."

"Of course."

Don't be preoccupied with the thought of "Is this when she tells him?" because I wasn't going to tell him. Or anyone else. For multiple reasons. On a psychoanalytical level, I didn't want to tell them because then I would have had to face it myself. If I didn't talk about it, then it wasn't real. I liked living in some version of denial, as I believed most Americans did. It was okay. My denial wasn't going to change my circumstance.

On another level, I wanted to see my friends as they were. I didn't want to see them scared, or panicked, or sad, or weirded out. Just as they felt, when they felt, what they felt. Maybe the sudden loss of a friend would be traumatizing, but I didn't need to add weeks of stress onto that. And lastly, maybe most importantly, I just wanted them to see me as I was. I didn't want them to look for things to corroborate that I was sick. I wanted to be me, here, fully

-- and then not.
So I would lie my ass off until this was all over.
This.
Life.

"You know, it was just something that happened. I don't think we need to think too deep into it. I don't want to. It's over, I'm alive. All's well."

"Okay," Shep said, unconvinced.

At the movie theater, Shepherd got us in with a wink to the kid behind the counter. I felt like he was almost walking in slow motion, which was oddly expected.

"What do you want?"

"I don't know. Popcorn?"

"Chet. Chet," he motioned over to yet another child worker and started pointing at things and talking slowly. He was like the damn Godfather of the movie theater.

It was ten o'clock in the morning. The first movie started at 10:30, and I hadn't seen another soul that wasn't wearing a bright blue polo shirt and a name tag. The parking lot was busy but that's because we were attached to the mall. There was low elevator music playing on the surround sound. There was a tall, bored-looking teenager sweeping invisible trash from the floor into a dustpan. And then there was me, feeling completely old, wondering why these kids weren't in school. What were they doing with their lives? Where were their parents?

A few minutes later, Chet came back to the counter with a giant popcorn, two large sodas, and enough candy to give an elephant diabetes.

Shepherd picked it all up and handed me a soda to carry. The payment for all of this inventory?

One single wink.

"How much would all this be?" I whispered.

"Don't worry about it," Shepherd told me, without moving his lips.

We went into the first theater of the day, the lights were still on, and it was empty. We used to love this. We used to love being in a theater, just the two of us. Fooling around and making out. Barely paying attention to whatever was on screen.

I didn't remember the feelings I felt for Shepherd, which would be too strange. But, I remembered the rushes I felt being around him. My heart used to pound out of it's chest. Sweaty hands, pulsing vageen -- I mean the whole thing. I thought he was so sweet and sexy and, honestly, that whole winking thing would've dropped my drawers back then.

He could have had it.

I knew where we were going as I climbed the stairs, following him up to our seats. Middle of the theater. Middle of the row.

There was something to be said about coming to the early movie.

"Which one are we seeing first?" I asked, knowing he wasn't going to tell me.

"Can you just be on the ride?"

I laughed, pretty sure I taught him that saying. We propped up our feet on the seats in front of us and dug into the unevenly salted popcorn.

"Remember when we came to see *Serendipity*?" I referenced my favorite John Cusack film, which was sandwiched between two others on a day like this a thousand years ago.

"God, I love that movie," he said. "We listened to that soundtrack every night."

"Every night," I repeated. "I still listen to it some days. When it's cold out."

"Yeah, it's great for Christmastime."

"It is."

We used to make out to that soundtrack in Shepherd's car. Neither of us said that. But if I was thinking it, I knew he was, too. An older couple walked in and sat in the front row. On cue, Shepherd and I rolled our eyes and groaned.

Why us?

Poor us.

We stopped and laughed at each other.

"Old habits," he said.

"Of all the movies, in all the world..." I started.

"Why'd they have to walk into this one?"

We cracked up at this cheesy inside joke and then, I sobered.

"Are you seeing anyone?" I asked, nearly making him choke on his popcorn.

"What? No -- why are you asking that now?"

"I haven't asked you yet."

"No, no I'm not. I don't really have time for a relationship."

"Between..."

"I don't really want a girlfriend, okay?"

He defensively shook his head and looked straight ahead.

"Okay."

We both faced forward for a few seconds before it got too awkward.

"You're a really good boyfriend," I told him. "You were the best boyfriend ever."

"God, that was forever ago. Do you know how weird that is to hear now?"

"No weirder than saying it. Just, if I didn't ever say it, or get to say it -- I'm saying it now. You could make a girl happy."

He nodded, his mouth twisted in embarrassment.

"Well, thank you for saying that."

"You're welcome...but, I mean it."

"I know you do."

"You don't KNOW that."

"I don't often hear you say things you don't mean."

There was this little space in my chest that I felt go soft and crack open a smidge. There it was. A piece of why I was here. I was recognized.

The lights dimmed and I settled down into my seat, snuggled up in my big sweater and next to the Cool Water I hadn't realized I'd missed.

Hmm, home.

"So, I really liked her and I thought it was all heading somewhere."

"I remember. I remember you telling me about her."

"Yeah, so we had that big tornado like an hour from here. Did you hear about that?"

"I don't know, tornadoes when you don't live around them all seem to be the same thing."

"Well, this one was really, really bad."

I cringed at the thought. Growing up in the Midwest, tornadoes were my worst nightmare, despite their pervasiveness. Texas had its fair share but the state was so vast, and they never came near Austin.

"Was there a baby?" I grimaced.

"What?"

"Was there a baby? You know, there's always a baby who gets thrown somewhere. Was there one this time? Was it okay?"

Shepherd started to chuckle, his shoulders bouncing up and down.

"I'm not trying to be funny! I'm genuinely hoping there wasn't."

"I'm pretty sure there was. And he was okay."

"Thank god. God, if babies could talk. I'd want to talk to one of the tornado-surviving ones. I'd be very curious to see what he'd have to say."

"Okay," he reminded me that he was the one talking. We were sitting in the second theater, waiting for the next movie to start, after sizable disappointment in the first one.

"Okay, sorry, the tornado and the girl."

"Kelsey."

"Kelsey."

"So, she goes down there to volunteer, clean, and salvage."

I clutched my hand to my chest.

"Awesome. So she's a sweetheart."

"Yup. Yup. Oh, heart of gold. And she calls me every night and fills me in on what's going on."

"And you didn't want to go down there with her and help?"

"No. No, you know -- my back. My knees. I can't."

"Mm-hm," I said, hoping I sounded the right amount of judgmental.

"So, anyway," he paused to take a sip of Sprite. "She calls me, like, the third night she's down there. And we're talking, and she's telling me about all the debris and how she's found pictures with the glass intact and baby toys, you know?"

"I can't imagine."

"No, it sounds terrible. See, you don't want to go down there, either. So, I ask her if she's found anything real weird."

"Like what? A dildo or some shit?" I said, blowing it off.

Shepherd's eyes got wide, and he started to hit the seat enthusiastically.

"This is it! THIS is why I love you. Yes. Yes. A dildo. That's exactly what I said! Did you find a dildo in the rubble?"

We both started cracking up because, of course, that's what he said. And he just yelled it again in his place of work.

"And she didn't think that was hilarious?"

"Hung up and I have never heard from her again."

I pulled my head back in shock.

"That's about her," I said, defensively and with terminology probably best reserved for other things.

"Right?"

"She clearly has a problem, with sex and jokes and that has nothing to do with you. Her loss."

"I knew you would get it, I was trying to make her feel better." I didn't mention that after days of seeing people at their lowest and most vulnerable, I probably wouldn't want my non-volunteering, almost-boyfriend joking around about it either, but I don't. True loyalty sometimes was just keeping your mouth shut.

"So, I don't know. I don't really want to date anyone. I'm happy the way I am."

"You don't want kids ever?"

"God, no, do you remember me with kids?"

"You're referring to farting on your nephew's head --" Shepherd giggled proudly.

"Yeah."

"You were a kid, too, then. I didn't know if you had changed your opinion."
I hoped I didn't sound encouraging. I was not encouraging Shepherd to procreate. I was just trying to prod a little deeper into his mind. Pull apart the pieces of old and the pieces of new in the ten minutes before the next movie.

"I have not. If anything, I moreso don't want kids. They're expensive, they're gross. I'd rather just take care of myself and, like I said, I'm not seeing anyone."

"Yeah, that would make it hard."

"You don't want kids do you?"

"No," I said. "I'm not going to have any."

"Yeah, you are so not mom material."

"No," I said, with a little laugh I was hiding behind. "Fuck no," I said more adamantly. "Fuck no, never," I said, so low I couldn't hear.

I spent the next two hours of this blockbuster action movie bawling my fucking eyes out softly, trying to hide it from Shepherd. I didn't know if it was me or this other part that took over sometimes.
The part that came with the thing.

Where I was laughing or screaming or crying with no harbinger, no reason. The part that flipped out at the bowling alley. The part that was insulted by not being "mom material." I didn't know if we were divinely connected, using one brain as a host -- or if we were fighting each other to take over and control my body. It was all very surreal up there, and I didn't have anything to compare it to. Other than the movie *Face/Off*.

Or maybe *The Mask*.

One of those movies where there was a big-chinned actor and you didn't know who was who, and there was a good guy and a bad guy fighting for the same turf. There were explosions and a hot chick and yeah -- it was really just like that.

# 15

## JAMES

I HAD THIS BOYFRIEND BACK IN AUSTIN.

On paper, I was dating up. Handsome guy, master's degree in Theology, liked to cook and made his own beer, worked out four times a week at least, loved foreign movies, blah, blah, blah.

What every girl said they wanted.

But does anyone really want that?

In play, those things added up to an annoying level of arrogance, and I was exhausted in his presence. The kind of guy that made you think he was okay with you not shaving your legs but really he was cringing and refusing to touch you in silent protest of them. He wasn't the guy that would say, "Shave your fucking legs... please, baby," like a human with needs. He would silently pick my legs up from resting over his, ankle by ankle, drop them to the ground and give this tight-lipped, disgusted half-smile while clearing his throat. And I'm not talking about hairy-beast, lost-in-the-wilderness legs -- I'm talking about four days. A week, tops?

I didn't know what I was doing. With him. James. You know what? I don't want you to know his real name. So forget I ever said it.

So, of course, of *course*, six weeks after I broke it off with {redacted}, I realized I hadn't had a period. I was working and traveling nonstop to keep my mind off things with him and by the time I had a second to slow down and breathe...uhh -- well there was a positive test involved. I was pro-choice, certain I never wanted kids and definitely not wanting any with him.
I made the appointment for an abortion. There was nowhere in my life for a child, and I wasn't willing to make the room. If I ever had one, it had to be with a man I trusted; despite their beautiful examples, I didn't want to be my mother, my grandmother. In that respect. I also didn't want to juggle schedules and have custody battles forever with someone I could barely stand. Parts of him. Parts of him, I couldn't stand. I wished the baby were Alex's. Then, we could make it work. I thought no matter whose baby I had, Alex would help make it work.

I had a week before I could get in. I tried to push it out of mind and pretend there was nothing happening there. But the fatigue took over, so I couldn't run. And the puking in the morning, sans hangover. Although I wasn't going to continue the pregnancy, I couldn't bring myself to drink during it, either. I could respect this creature's life until it was over. I told myself not to get attached. Didn't look at apps. Didn't look up blogs. I knew what I wanted. Didn't backtrack.
It was my dreams that betrayed me.

It showed up.
In rapid succession: all my fears and hopes.
A flash. Josephine's eyes.
A set of feet running barefoot through a hall.

An inch of death.
Me and Alex.
The tubes.
I was puking.
My hair on the ground.
Baby laughter.
A kick
A rapid heartbeat.
The taste of death.
Blood.
I was screaming. I was beating someone up.
Yellow roses.
A baby's cry.
Fire.
The sound of a mommy.
And a much younger me.
The scent of death.
Tiny fingers.

I woke up in cold sweats.
I shook my head -- I couldn't. I wouldn't change my mind. This was my mind and my body. So, I could have changed it, if I wanted to. I could have called {redacted} and filled him in. I could have started there. Nothing would change my mind. But it was a start.

He said no. Simple as that. There was no more explanation. He wasn't interested in being a father. Oh. They just got to say that, and it was done. Even nature's fucked with double standards.
A flash of Josephine and Kim ran through my head. They did it. Would I have ended it all? I was the only one left. {redacted} didn't deserve our bloodline. But neither had my sperm-donor father. We could have continued on.

I imagined the next little woman, and this one looked like me. Kim got to love her the way Jose loved me. We were all we ever had. She could be part of that. I thought there were people who loved me, but there were only two people I could prove it to be true. True and unconditional. I wouldn't mind more love.

I woke up writhing in chills, teeth chattering, blood pouring through the mattress and down my legs.

When Alex came home, he found me sobbing in bed, curled up fetal, and hidden under the mounds of heavy blankets and pillows I'd placed on me so they felt as heavy as a person. I heard him drop his things at the arch of my bedroom door, and I tried to buck up and stop the wailing that was feeling so radically right. Hanging on to my cell phone, waiting for someone to magically call me.
Text me some loving words.
But no one knew.
No one would ever have guessed.

He came into my bed and wrapped himself around me. He put his face on my face and laced an arm underneath me and cradled it to the shape of my body.
He pulled me in as tight as two separate people could be and gave me all of the permission in the world to let go.
He stayed with me while I did. Every raw, aching second of it.
My hairy legs wrapped right around his.

Four months later, I was standing in the line of a fucking Subway sandwich shop.

# 16

## Under the Water and Over the Moon

Every Tuesday and Thursday morning my mom was gone when I woke up. She came home around 11:30 and jumped directly into the shower, avoiding me.

One day, when she came out, I greeted her at the door.

"Do you have a boyfriend?"

"God, no, come on."

"Where were you? What do you do on these mornings?"

"Honey, I don't have to tell you everything.'

Kim was a creature of habit.

A loosey-goosey, unpredictable type of habit. When she was gone on Saturdays, I knew she was at a thrift store hunting for shit she didn't need. When she was gone on Sundays, I knew she was at church. When she was gone in the afternoons, I knew she was at t'ai chi.

Her empty nest syndrome led her to some interesting hobbies, which she loved talking about. Usually, she couldn't wait to come home and tell me about her day.

It was for that reason I became obsessed with these absent, secretive mornings of hers. Showers, when taken out of context, could be alarming. Mom had every right to go where she wanted, do what she wanted. Literally, every right.

It was just that -- I had to fucking know! She had the rest of her life for secrets.

Monday night I began to plan my ruse.

On the outside, I was tending to a new crossword puzzle; on the inside, I was scheming ways to invade my mother's privacy.

"I am so tired, Mom," I forced a yawn.

"You should get some rest, baby girl."

"I think I'll call it a night. I'm going to get up early for a run."

"Are you sure? Maybe you should take it easy."

I put my master plan on its feet.

"I don't know, I'll try. If my door is closed, I didn't go and don't wake me."

She scrunched her face: offended by my projection that she would disturb me.

"Okay, I'll be home around 11:30."

"Oh yeah, I forgot you have your thing tomorrow." Sly as a fox.

"Mm-hm."

"Your secret gun club?"

"Nope."

"Scrapbooking League?"

"Sure," she batted her eyes at me.

I kissed her and headed upstairs, ready to put part two into action.

A good night's rest.

I woke up the first time I heard Mom's alarm go off. I knew she'd snooze it twice, which gave me time to sneak out of the house and into her car. My life must have been horribly boring.

I rifled through the back seats and found a cozy space just about my size in the midst of hundreds of miscellaneous items. I piled some blankets on top of me. She would never know. I started to question why I was doing this again, but it was too late to not do it. I hunkered down in my spot, surrounded by the smell of old things, and tried for the most comfortable position possible. It wasn't bad. Cozy, really.

I would have killed for this as a kid. Of course, I also failed by not bringing snacks.

The sound of the engine woke me from my dozing. Oh my god, I was really doing this. I was really this fucking bored. Mom beat on the steering wheel to sounds of the seventies. I heard her mumble dissatisfaction with the traffic, was shifted by two sharp turns, and, after ten minutes, she parked. I waited until she climbed out and I could hear her footsteps walking away before I looked up.

A strip mall.

Of course.

I squinted to find her before I lost her in a random store. The one she went into didn't have a permanent sign. When she disappeared, I left the car and stealthily made my way behind her.

The overwhelming odor of chlorine hit before I even entered. When I did, the smell was accompanied by the sounds of splashing, whistles, and the boing of a diving board. A girl at the front desk greeted me, asking if she could help. I was stymied.

"Um, maybe? Did my mother just walk in here?"

"Umm, I don't know who your mother is?"

"Right...right," I stared past her, watching a man as smooth as a dolphin bounce twice from a high diving board and enter the water with Olympic precision.

"I'm sorry," I shook my head. "What is this place?"

"The Aquatic Center."

"As in water?"

She nodded slowly, clearly concerned about my cognition.

"Kim," I told her. "Kim Douglas."

"Oh, yes! She's so funny. She's in the advanced scuba training."

I squinted my eyes to understand what her words meant.

"Scuba?"

"Yes. Self-Contained Underwater --"

"I know what scuba means," I interjected. "Can I go see her? She forgot something."

"Sure. Just sign in here and through those doors."

*My* head was swimming. I felt like I was underwater without an apparatus. Kim didn't do water. Water and heights. No way. These were the things I knew for sure about her. I stalked into the pool area like I was going to retrieve her and bring her back to her senses. She spied me first, walking straight toward me, in a full-on wetsuit. My eyes bulged. Her eyes bulged. And then we became one.

"What are you doing here?" we both yelled.

We both calmed down. We both exhaled and then, Mom repeated:

"Jorah, what are you doing here?"

"I followed you. Why are you wearing that?"

She paused, her face brilliantly framed by the tight black surround of the suit.

"I am training, okay?"

She crossed her arms and tapped her foot, equal parts embarrassed and furious. I wasn't welcome.

"I'm going to go," she turned away.

"Mom, wait," I called after her. "I'm sorry." I dropped my voice so she wouldn't be worried about other people hearing us.

"Why are you here?" she nearly hissed.

"I thought I'd come and see what you do these days you don't want to talk about."

She was biting her lip and jostling her leg.

"Mom, I'll leave. I'll go wait outside until you're done. I didn't think this would be a big deal. I thought we'd get a laugh --"

"Just go wait for me in the car," she cut me off. "I'll leave early to get you home."

"No, please don't. Stay. I'll wait."

I noticed, then, a tall, middle-aged man walking over to us, also in a wetsuit. He waved in our direction.

Amazing masculine figure, slicked-back silver hair, strong jaw, and, as he came closer, incredible gray eyes. I looked at Mom, suspiciously.

Mo-om.

*Tell me this is what you're doing.*

"Kim!" he called. She turned beet red, looking for an exit.

He stopped in front of us, flippers and all, dripping wet with a smile that blinded.

"Hi. Hi, Laith," she timidly greeted him.

Laith. I swooned for my mother, who was just trying to hold it together.

I was a grade-A asshole impeding her getting her groove back.

"I wanted to catch up with you and talk about this weekend; is it a bad time?"

Mom looked at me, and I wished I could melt into a little Alex Mack puddle and slip on out of there.

"I'll just go wait in the car," I said, nodding to them like a subservient.

"Hi, I'm Laith," he stuck out his strong and wide hand for me to shake. I gave my mom a furtive glance and took it.

"Hi, I'm --"

"Laith," Mom breathed deeply. "This is my daughter. The one I'm always talking about. She followed me here."

"Actually, I rode WITH her, without her knowledge."

"Oh my goodness, your mother *loves* you."

I was taken aback by this ice breaker. I mean, of course she did.

"It's such a pleasure to meet you in person. She speaks of you so highly. I mean, I thought I loved my kids. So you are going to Australia with her?"

Huh?

I looked over at Mom, who was ready to hang herself to get out of that conversation.

"You're going to Australia?" I asked too loudly, nearly blowing her weak cover. She put her head down and gave me the eye to be "in" on this.

"Oh -- oh!" I recovered. "I'm thinking of the New Zealand leg, that's what I've been calling it."

"Yeah," Laith was none the wiser. "You two are going to have a blast down there. I mean, some of the best beaches, best water of my life."

"Well, Mom's the expert there, so I'll just let her lead the way," I extended an olive branch. I excused myself with a fake phone call and left them to their wetsuits.

When we got into the car, I felt ashamed. I interrupted her life. She was so silent it hurt.

"Mom, I'm so sorry," I said first. "I didn't know I was ruining anything. I was trying to be funny."

"You were being nosy."

"And that."

"If I wanted you to know what I do here, then all of those times you asked I would have just told you."

Damn.

Mom logic can be airtight.

"I didn't think of it like that."

She breathed in so deep that it was loud and visible, her hands on the steering wheel, eyes focused on nothing.

"It's okay. It's okay -- now you know."

"Why did you want to hide scuba lessons?"

"It was just something I wanted to do for me. You get a certain age and you think it's too late to try new things."

"You're not old at all."

"I know that. I realized it wasn't me talking -- it was society, telling me I was too old. And. You know, life's too short," she looked at me, "no matter how old you are. So I wanted to try this out. And I love it."

"And Laith?"

"Laith," she spilled a little moonlight in her voice. "Laith is a friend. He's very sweet."

"Very hot."

"He's attractive."

"You come here to see him."

"I think it's mutual. It didn't start that way. We both were here to try it out."

"He's single?"

"Yes."

"Boyfriend alert," I sang.

"No, no way. I don't know when I'll be able to date someone."

I knew that sentiment was about me, but I didn't want it to be.

"He likes you."

"I think I like him, too."

Her copper face was alight with blush. Her lips were pursed in an embarrassed but flattered way, which I was sure she gave Laith all the time.

"You deserve so much love, Mama."

"Thanks, babe."

She didn't really look at me, just stared straight ahead.

"What's all this Australian business? You shouldn't lie to make a guy like you," I laughed and watched her smirk turn dark. She dipped her eyes down and then back up to me.

"I am going to Australia. It's on my bucket list, and I'm going."

I felt my head explode, and koalas popped out. Where to start?

"Kangaroos?" I accidentally said.

"Yes."

I tried to start over with an actual question.

"You have a bucket list?"

"I do, indeed. What do you think I'm taking all these classes for? You think I WANT to do t'ai chi?"

"Well, that's what a bucket list is for, things you want to do."

"Mine is more like things I thought I wanted to do and then got there and wanted to leave, but I already paid."

I threw my head back laughing and Mom giggled along, basking in the moment.

"Well, when are you going to Australia? I'd like to see what else is on your list."

"December," she said solemnly.

"Oh."

"But I don't know," she rushed. "Things change. So..."

The levity broke way for the tension of reality. She was going on a trip with me. To take me there. To leave parts of me there. And we both knew it, but I didn't want to know it. So I kept going.

"And you're going to scuba dive?"

"I am going to, maybe, attempt to snorkel and work my way up from there. Oxygen doesn't stay in the body the same way after forty-five, so I'm high risk."

"Oh please, James Cameron's old ass can't stay out of the water. You'll be fine. You'll be perfect."

That was the first time my mother had acknowledged that there would be life without me. There would be a lot of it. Loads of it. Planes full of it. Continents full of it.

There was an old song on the radio. The dash was maroon leather and the seats were almost velvet.

It was just starting to feel like afternoon instead of morning.

Mom hadn't started the car yet but wouldn't take her hands off the wheel.

I was jealous.
I wanted to go to Australia.
I wanted a bucket list.
I wanted her life.

# 17
## The Tubes

You said you were going to be here by now. I feel like a soap opera repeating the same lines over and over to you. To your voicemail! I sound like a WIFE!"

I furiously pushed the end call button on my phone and sent it flying across the bed.

Maybe he wasn't coming. He was scared. I knew he was scared; I knew he was busy. But, that was the plan.

I wanted to understand where his mind was, but it felt impossible. I had always come first. And now, when I needed him the most, it was like catching a phantom thing. Couldn't he feel me anymore?

*I need you here you selfish bastard.*

*Get here and do what the fuck you said you were going to do.*

My mind began screaming. Screaming so loud I was sure my tumor heard it.

FUCK YOU!

I screamed again, just for it. Special delivery -- I hoped you heard me. I hoped they heard it all the way to Texas.

When it all first happened I thought I had picked up a parasite or virus. West Nile or some other dangerous fad disease.
Dry mouth, light shaking. I wasn't understanding some words, my tongue was tripping on other ones.
It felt like there was water in my head. Rushing, sloshing waves between my ears. Sometimes a dull siren. I checked WebMD easily over a hundred times; I had eighteen diseases, but I didn't mention it.
I remembered a day when I couldn't wake up.
My whole body had become an anvil covered by skin and my eyes were magnets sinking into the heavy metal. I was lethargic and groggy and could barely move.
The curtains couldn't open because the light made me want to die and when I tried to go pee, my knees were weak underneath me.
You know...
The flu. Umm...food poisoning. An off day.
I took over-the-counter meds and stayed in bed, battling the call of my responsibilities.
I'd be better in the morning.

Then I had my first seizure.
So, seizures were like one of those things you grew up hearing about and you kind of understood. Like, someone started shaking and foaming at the mouth, and you'd better hope they weren't driving.
Like, you knew about seizures. I figured I did. I never really gave them a second thought.

I was in line at a fucking Subway sandwich shop, of all places. Trying to take charge of my life and order the perfect sandwich expediently.

No pickles. Heavy mayo. Tuscan Wheat. And, in a split second, my life was divided into before and after.

I didn't remember much.  It was a bright white flash, like may have been expected.

I was pointing at the mustard. I was very decisive.

"No, none of that. Absolutely zero mustard," I said it so self-assured: the most important communication of the day.

I said it like "chop chop."

And next, I was on the floor staring into the faces of strangers. Their voices sounded like water. I was being lifted into an ambulance with an oxygen mask and no answers.

I wasn't scared. I remembered being curious.

Really, angrily and gratefully curious.

*What the fuck am I doing here? But, thank you for taking care of me.*

Like that.

When I woke up the next time, I was in a hospital bed, plugged into an IV, with a nurse asking me questions. Well, I had questions for her, too.

"Did someone get my sandwich?"

She smiled and laid my head back with a firm hand.

"I don't think so. Who should we call? We need to call your family."

"Do NOT call my mother," I tried to sit up, but considered the dull throb pulsing through my head and the bandage wrapped around it.

"My mother is in Nebraska and she can't get here and she would freak out. What's going on? Did I fall?"

"You did fall. You suffered a seizure."

"I seized?" I yelled, in the throes of utter confusion. There had to be some mistake. I didn't seize.

"You did. You had a tonic-clonic seizure and you fell. You hit your head on the ground when you did that. One of the customers knew to put his belt between your teeth and called 911. They took care of you."

"Someone put a belt in my mouth?"

I thought back to the people in line with me.

"Tell me it wasn't the homeless guy."

She stifled a reaction.

"I don't know. But you were lucky he did it."

I lifted my hands to my head and tried to collect my sparse and jumbled thoughts. I heard the beeping of my heart monitor -- measured, tiny blips. I freaked out.

"I need Alex. I need to call Alex," my breath was short.

"Is that your husband?"

I nodded frantically without correcting her. She asked me for his number.

"I want him here now," I pressed, and she exited the room hastily to make the call.

I was surreal.

I was confused.

There was an older woman in line, too; they had us mistaken. We were switched. Something was wrong.

The nurse came back in and gave me my phone.

"Your husband is on the way," she said, and she touched my hand with hers. She must be new. I heard doctors and nurses were desensitized the longer they were on the job. But she was still gentle and soft.

"Do you have insurance?"

"Like health insurance?"

"Yes."

"Can I wait for my husband to get here?"

"Of course. Dr. Dickey will be in soon, he's going to want to talk to you about some tests and maybe run an MRI."

"What is that? The tube?"

"It is."

Alex ran into my room, looking every bit the worried husband. His breath was quick, his eyes saucers.

"Hey, hey, hey," he kissed my bandages."What is going on here?"

"I don't know," I grabbed his hand and held onto it. "They said I had a seizure."

"I know."

"Someone put a belt in my mouth and then they want me to get some tests. I don't know what's happening. I'm not thinking right. My brain feels --" all words escaped.

"It's okay, it's okay. I can ask all the questions."

"They asked me about health insurance."

Alex reached for his wallet.

"I brought it."

"We're so grown up."

"You're fucking lucky," Alex's voice dropped. "I got it before I knew plastic surgery wasn't covered."

"What were you going to do?"

"You know I wanted those pec implants."

"I thought that was a phase."

"It was, but, if insurance covered it, I would have gotten it done."

"Why would that be covered?"

The nurse came back before Alex could say anything, which was fine with both of us.

"Hi, you must be the husband."

"I am," he said it so easily I almost remembered our wedding day. "What is going on? I'm so worried," Alex kept hold of my hand.

"Your wife suffered a seizure, we're going to keep her overnight for monitoring. The doctor wants to conduct a scan."

"Of course, of course," Alex said and handed her the insurance card. "Whatever you need."

He handed it to her like it was a black American Express that got us into anywhere.

She left us alone again.

"How are you feeling?" he turned to me, sitting at my side.

"Stupid. I feel like I gave myself a seizure."

"What does that mean?"

"Where did this come from? Was I not drinking enough water? I don't remember the last time I worked out...like my body is shutting down around me. And yours probably is, too."

"Why mine?"

"Because we live the same. If I survive this we're turning it all around. Everything. Diet, exercise, booze, everything."

"Obviously you're going to survive it."

"So get ready to sweat."

A light, courteous knock rapped on the door, followed by the entrance of a tall, distinguished man. He was weathered, but handsome. His eyes didn't seem desensitized. He was reading my chart and probably knew more about me than I did.

"Dr. David Dickey, very nice to meet you both," he shook both of our hands and looked us directly in the eyes. His presence immediately brought another level of formality to the room. He stiffened up, and we braced ourselves. I was so glad Alex was there to listen. The overhead lighting was starting to blind me again, and I was going in and out of a mindful state.

"So, how are you?" Dr. Dickey asked, scooting a stool closer.

"Less and less like myself," I answered, as honestly as possible.

"Was that your first one?"

"I have never had anything like this happen to me ever," the more I spoke, the more timid was my voice. I was frightened.

"So. We're going to take you in for some blood tests and an MRI. We want a closer look at what is going on in that head of yours."

"Could you take some notes for me, doc? I never know," my husband laughed. Dr. Dickey gave a mere chuckle. He'd probably heard it all before.

*Put another stitch in for me, doc.*

*Take my wife, please!*

He was probably exhausted from bad husband jokes.

"I'd like to get that scan today, as soon as possible."

"Okay," I muttered.

"Do you have any questions for me?"

"Did the homeless guy put his belt in my mouth?"

They put me in the tube machine.

As they laid me down, I couldn't help but wonder how much that all would cost. I should have been having more selfish thoughts maybe. Like, why the fuck was I seizing? Did I need to give up red meat? But having never been in a room with anything so clearly expensive, the only thing I could think of was money.

I was alone. The doctors were on the other side of the wall, looking at screens that would give them answers. I didn't know that because they explained it to me, I knew it because of *Grey's Anatomy.*

*I wonder if there's a McDreamy here.*

*Maybe there's one in every hospital.*

*I bet there's a baby being born right...now.*

I was thinking of every mundane thing to avoid freaking out. But, I was lying in a vulnerable position on a conveyor belt carrying me into a hole. As I moved all the way in, I wished I'd called my mother.

Dr. Dickey said the scan could take from ten minutes to an hour, depending on what they found. The machine whirred around me and then went silent, in five-minute intervals, while I busied myself with stupid thoughts to drown out all the serious ones.

"People seize everyday, all over bullshit," I rapped in the style of T.I. I tapped my toes. I planned a party. I pretended I was in space. I was Sandra Bullock in *Gravity*, abandoned in millions of miles of nothing. So, maybe I was more George Clooney. But either way, I was in space. It was endless and deep and full of edges and meteors and heavens. I could see planets. Asteroids zoomed past. The sun. And the earth.

And then I thought if space was space then where could heaven be? If there was one. And how could the billions and trillions of people who have ever, ever lived fit in it if there was just one? That's when I convinced myself there wasn't one. There couldn't be a heaven because all those people couldn't fit. And if there wasn't one, where the hell was my grandmother?

Was she nowhere?

Was she floating around in space like George Clooney? And what did that mean for me?

What if something was wrong?

What if I was next?

What if I was just out there floating around, too, and we tried to find each other and we screamed and we reached out for each other, but we got sucked into our own private black holes and it was like we never existed to each other? The blood and genes and matching smiles and recipes meant nothing -- never were, never would be again.

How long had I been in there?

The machine was getting tighter around my still body, and I couldn't tell the difference between what was really happening and my space thoughts.

I would never see my grandmother again. She never existed, and I wouldn't exist, either.

Dr. Dickey said ten minutes to an hour. I had been in there way longer than ten minutes, so what were they looking at? What were they finding? The machine was screaming at me -- it was laughing. It heard my wild brain, and it dug deeper.

It knew what it was doing. I kicked my legs at it. I whipped my head from side to side, trying to shake out the horrible sound. The feeling of it, oozing out of my ears. It was not enough, it didn't listen. It still screamed. I reached my forearms as high as they would go, trying to break free from the plastic white wraps that held me down. I shook my head violently as the tube caved in.

"Dr. Dickey," I screamed, my own voice bumping off the sides of the tube and landing with hard jabs in my ears. The sound would never get out and back to him. It was in here trapped with me. My brain scans were red with anger and black with fear by then.

"Dr. Dickey!" I tilted my chin up and kicked my legs.

"Alex!" I tried again, knowing if anyone would ever hear me it would and could be him.

The machine shut down around me, the loud, laughing whir gone. There was only silence and the resonance of my yells reverberating in my mind. Had I been screaming? Was that me?

There was a shift, and I could see the ceiling of the room come into view as I slowly moved out of the tube.

What would I say? Had I ruined it all?

The tears fell as naturally as the screams; I couldn't fight them. My mouth curved into an ugly thing, and I wanted my mother more than ever. Alex, more than ever.

Dr. Dickey and the nurse were standing over me when I appeared. He was distressed, and the nurse tried to quickly untie me. But it wasn't quick enough.

"Get me out of here," I said wearily -- not angrily.

Dr. Dickey's face was furrowed and alarming. Whatever came next was going to be worse than the tube. I had a gut feeling.

I immediately questioned my ability to handle bad news. I just wanted to run. The nurse freed my arms, and I jumped from the bed, feeling stupid and dramatic.

"What happened?" Dr. Dickey asked.

"I can't possibly be the only person who ever lost it in one of those things."

"You're not. But what happened for you?"

"I just -- didn't like it," I muttered sheepishly. "Did you get what you needed?"

"We did. We did indeed. Hannah is going to take you back to the room and we'll go over your diagnosis."

A lump fell from my throat to my gut at the "d" word.

Diagnosis.

Diagnosis wasn't "fine." It wasn't "nothing." It was something. It was something bad -- that needed attention.

That we needed to go into the other room for.

I followed Hannah out. Alex was outside the door, waiting for me.

"There's a diagnosis," I whispered to him. His face turned long and white behind his beard.

"Did he say?"

"He's going to meet us in the other room."

He reached over and laced his fingers through mine, and we walked down the long, harsh lighting of the hospital hallway.

# 18

## SpiritCycle

I had given in to Stassi's earnest request to join her at SpiritCycle. I wasn't excited about it, but it meant a lot to her, and I wasn't against it. I knew to expect a hybrid of new age workout fads.

A mantra or affirmation. Someone weeping audibly in the back row. References to *The Secret*.

A year ago, I might have referenced it myself.

But there was something about the *thing* that made me lose all connection with the next level. Whatever you wanted to call it. For some people, sickness brought them closer to the light. I thought I would have been one of those people, when it was all hypothetical. Removed from me, I had it all figured out. The truth was, the only place I felt comfortable was in my insular, flawed, insane human mind. The spirit world, I wanted to stay far from.

I remembered well the last time I felt a moment of spirituality. Trail running in woods outside of Austin. Feet crunching before I could count my steps. Deer running on either side of me.

The sky filtered through the canopy. I swiped my arm across a broken branch and it cut me.

I finished my run holding my hand over my arm. When I finally stopped, I noticed the sticky blood falling through my fingers and pooling in the crevices.

A week later, those woods were ablaze with a fire started by some idiot who didn't know what dry season was. The dead wood and droughted land went up like a firecracker. I watched from the TV and could smell it in the air. My hand went to the place I'd been cut. A small piece of me was in that fire being sent into the sky.

A smoky funeral. Part of that forest forever in me. Leaving a scar.

I'd never felt so close to the earth.

And, I supposed, close to the spirit world.

Or whatever.

Where. Ever.

The SpiritCycle building was unextraordinary.

A four-room structure rife with energy and exclamation points. I followed Stassi in and watched her eagerly search the room.

"What are you looking for?"

"Just some friends."

I nodded and fell back into my strictly visiting role.

Surveying the posters on the concrete block walls. The gallons of protein next to tank tops for high prices.

The runner in me cringed, feeling confined. There'd be no forest fire here.

"Hi!" Stassi bounced up to the front desk.

"Hey. Are you here for SpiritCycle?"

Stassi flipped her hair and her giggle increased.

She was consistent in poorly flirting with the world.

"You know it. It's what I do. You've seen me around. I brought a friend today. Girl gang!"

She ended that by uncomfortably clearing her throat. The girl behind the counter barely noticed, she nodded politely and focused on the screen. Checking us in.

"There they are."

Stassi pointed to the door, eying it intensely. Three women, nearly girls, stood there talking. Tall and lean, wearing half tops and short shorts.

"Who are they?"

"Friends of mine. Kind of. They come here, too."

"Do you want to go say hi?"

"NO," Stassi grabbed my wrist, holding me in place.

"We're not friend friends."

"Not the kind of friends who say hi," I clarified.

"No."

Instead of greeting them, Stassi assumed the position of totem pole. Scrunching her shoulders in, and her chin back until it was doubled, she widened her smile across her face and waved at them. From the elbow to the shoulder, nothing moved. The forearm and hand waved frantically.

They nodded in recognition that she was indeed there.

"They're just the coolest. They're so pretty. I mean, really pretty. They're model pretty."

"You're staring."

She averted her eyes to an awkward place on the floor.

A welcoming brunette greeted me with a shoulder touch.

"Hi, you're new to class?"

"I am, yes. Jorah."

"Heather. Great to see a new face. If you need anything please ask me, or one of the ladies over there. Stassi, you too, of course."

Heather pointed in the direction of three other women. Cute women. With fanny packs and t-shirts.

I waved and they waved back.

Stassi did not wave.

"We may go out for caffeine after class, you're welcome to join."

"Thank you so much."

Heather returned to her group.

"They're really sweet," I turned to Stassi.

"It's the mom group," she said with disdain. "Booooring."

"You're a boring mom, though."

"They're just not my type," she whispered through a grimace. "They all have short hair and who knows what else. Anyway, when I'm here, I'm not a mom. I'm just Stassi. Hanging out. Getting my Zen on."

"Alright, I'm just here for *your* ride."

"I think me and those girls have a lot more in common than me and the moms anyway. I hear them talk. We like the same things. They're so funny. They go out with guys. All things I used to do."

"As long as you don't actively discuss it with them."

"Jorah, conversation is so yesterday."

I agreed with that and dropped it.

We walked into the dark room and felt our way to the seats of the spinning bikes.

They were thin and sleek. The room was musty with Nag Champa and old sweat. We weren't the first class of the day. People filed in and found their own sexy bikes. The girls sat in the row in front of us. Stassi peacocked.

"We should really go out tonight," she asserted, with an odd vocal fry. "I HAVE to get out."

"Um, okay. I would."

"Don't you feel like dancing? I want to hit a club."

I hoped that Stassi sensed my disdain for the charade. A few short weeks before, I might have humored her. I would have jumped in and played my role to help her befriend the it crowd.

But not today. Not ever again.

There were still lessons to be learned in what time was left and also lessons to be taught. A primary one, an overdue one, was that of skin. I wanted, for many years, for Stassi to be comfortable in her own. I assumed it longed to be stretched to the bones by its inhabitant. To merge. That was all skin really wanted: I thought, to be made comfortable in. A perfect fit with the soul, mind, body of its person.

Stassi's skin ached with the expectations of others. Pulled in odd directions. Didn't have clothes to fit it.

I imagined her skin stayed up most nights, unable to sleep, wondering when Stassi would return for it.

The girl it knew when she was born. When she was a small child, learning the world, scraping its knee, and blissfully living.

Without the pretense of society or family.

Natural. Authentic. Her skin wasn't made to keep up with the Joneses or the cool girls.

It was made for her to be easy in.

It was waiting for her to accept it as it was. I thought that much of skin's longing had to do with honesty, and there were so few willing to be honest with themselves -- they would never fit it.

"Stassi, we haven't been to a club in ages."

"Speak for yourself," she threw out, silently pleading me to join in.

The girls weren't listening. They were talking among themselves, their skins -- for the moment -- breathing easy. They weren't rude. They weren't anything. They were strangers enjoying their day.

"Why are you doing this?" I gave in, unable to participate. "Why are you trying to impress them?"

Stassi's face caved in, deep with embarrassment. She looked for words, and her head shook back and forth.

"Stassi," I kept my voice low. "They don't care. They are just here to pedal. And so are you."

"I really don't like you right now. If it's not your idea you shit on it."

There was a lull in the girls' conversation and one of them looked back at us, to make certain she heard correctly.

"You don't like you. And that's the whole point."

The words flew from my cerebral cortex, off my tongue, and into the universe so fast, it broke light.

It rolled out so easy, we both recognized it as at least partially true.

Stassi sat back like she'd been slapped. I immediately kind of regretted it.

"That's not what I meant," I started. "You should just be yourself?" I reverted back to the old standby.

"Maybe you just don't know me that well."

The instructor galloped to the front of the class.

A slight, muscular man. He lit candles on a table next to his bike.

He smudged sage around us in a frame.

"Namaste," he began, the first of many appropriated Sanskrit terms.

*OM-mygod, I feel good.*

*Glad you got your ASANA to class today.*

Stassi faced straight ahead, determined to ignore me.

Out-pedal everyone.

I could see the set in her jaw: it was tight and focused. Polar opposite of mine. I wavered in and out of his mantras. Pedaling hard and then barely at all.

"You can reach the sky!"

*I can reach the sky.*

"You are the only obstacle in your life."

*She has to know how dumb it makes her look.*

"Your life is a miracle."

*Why do I care how dumb she looks? Why is it my business?*

"You can achieve anything."

*I can achieve anything.*

When the class finished, I glanced at Stassi, hoping she had worked through her hatred. She had already exited the room, her bike still wet where her body touched it. I wiped it down and filed out with other slow movers. Stassi was there talking to the tall girls. Neck leaning all the way up, for a view of their glistening under chins.

I didn't approach. I held back, in earshot, on needles.

Stassi's too keen laugh filled the lack of talking points, too interested to be interesting.

"I just love your looks. Maybe after a few more classes, I'll be wearing a crop top, too," Stassi put her hands on her wide hips and swiveled them.

The whole room tightened.

Or maybe just my anus.

"Maybe," one of them said, laughing and noncommittal.

"So we're going to grab chai, maybe we'll see you next time." They attempted a move toward the door.

"Chai? I love chai. It's my favorite caffeine. I didn't know you guys drank chai! I would have totally invited you for some."

She searched back for me, smugly.

A "See, bitch?" look.

"Did...you want to join us now?" one of them asked cautiously, hoping not to be too inviting. How people spoke when they just wanted to be with friends. Not editing their language for strangers.

Stassi stepped on her tiptoes, her fingers tingled with excitement.

Victory?

"Do I ever! Ugh, but I have somebody with me," she thumbed in my direction.

Somebody's direction.

I could feel her eyes rolling. Her voice dropped; my ears strengthened.

"She's tagging along, she's from...Texas," her voice sounded like a cracked egg. She could barely say the T-word.

One of their faces brightened and caught my eye. She waved me over.

"What part of Texas? I just graduated UT."

"I went to UT," I pressed my palm to my heart, coming closer. Simultaneously, we threw up Hook 'em Horns. We both grabbed each other's fingers and started laughing with that common bond of shared teachers, buildings, and school bars between us. Stassi also threw up a Hook 'em.

"Did you go to Texas, too?" the girl asked, in the throes of more excitement.

"No, I stayed here," her fingers still in the air.

The girl cocked her head, like a confused puppy.

"Stassi, that sign is the school signal. For the Longhorns."

The girls all stifled a laugh and I decidedly did not. Stassi lowered her hand and rubbed it protectively.

"I thought you guys were just saying rock and roll."

"Ha! No," my schoolmate laughed a little too mockingly. The *faux pas* had become a way out.

"It's not like you graduated, Jorah," Stassi tried to pass that off as a joke. "Can you do horns if you didn't graduate?"

She chuckled as though we were supposed to join in too. I definitely wasn't.

"Well, we're leaving. Hey, we should get together and talk Austin," she said to me. "You coming to class again?"

"Uh, maybe. Probably," I lied.

"Okay, I'll catch up with you. Texas Fight!"

"Texas Fight!"

I could barely look at Stassi.

"Thank you for making me look like an idiot," she hissed again, her eyes down.

"I did what? How?"

"Correcting me in front of them. You just had to take over the conversation and make me look like a fool."

"You didn't need me to make you look like a fool, Stass."

"I think I'm starting to see why so many people have a problem with you, honestly."

She turned her back and headed out the glass doors.

I stayed nonplussed.

What people?

# 19

## The Date

Mom had accepted her first date in two decades. Maybe more.

Laith had generously offered to take her out on the town and "show her around" the city she'd grown up in. How charming of him. She said yes, but she was skittish. Sweaty hands when she hung up the phone.

"I need you to come with me," she pleaded. "I can't do this alone."

"Mom, that's weird."

"I don't want to give him the wrong impression."

My eyes squinted.

"What does that mean to you? Because you CAN go out with him and not put out."

"I don't know what we'll talk about."

"There's a universe of things to talk about."

"I haven't done this in a lifetime."

"It's going to be okay."

"You owe me."

"Mom."

"I'm cashing in. It will make me more comfortable for you to be there."

"It will make your date way less comfortable."

"You can bring Shepherd, it will be a double," she was pacing. Her fingers twitched, and I could sense her tunnel vision. "Then there will be four of us. And the conversation will flow better with four of us. It's good."

"Mom," I whined, again.

"Call Shep," her voice was stern. She turned and flipped from the room, leaving me in my solitary disapproval.

I supposed it would be a good thing to learn more about Laith. Watching Mom maneuver her way through a night with a handsome man might have been fun.

I could vet him. Save her time, if he was the wrong one.

And I did owe her. She had never cashed in on anything I'd owed her before.

I dialed Shep, out of Mom's earshot, thinking of how I could make this fun.

"Hey, you," the sweetness in my voice caught him off-guard.

"Hey...Jorah?"

"Yeah," I continued, like honey. "What are you doing tonight?"

"I uh -- uh. I --" he stammered, making me laugh. "Why are you talking like that? I don't have anything going on tonight."

"Well, you do now," I paused for effect. "How would you like to go on a date with me?"

The back of my neck prickled. My mouth twitched with a giggle breaking through.

Shepherd was silent and then cleared his throat.

"Umm, like what kind of date?"

"Like a dinner date. A wine-and-candles date. The date we never got as kids."

I pulled the phone from my face, lurching with a belly laugh. I covered my mouth and stifled my breathing.

I would pay to see his face. Red as hell. Oafish, uncertain.

"Oh, wow. I am. Flattered. I am so flattered. Um, the thing is, you know, we go way back..." Shep bumbled on.

"You were my first love, Shep."

"Yeah, yeah. I just don't know if we'd be compatible. I mean, you are so -- flattering..."

I rolled my eyes and continued.

"We're compatible. My fire to your..." I lost my analogy and let it drift off into the ether.

"This is unbelievable," he said under his breath.

"I'll always love you," he said to me, in a voice more serious than expected.

I waited for him to follow that with a "but." It didn't come. Or it took too long to emerge. The words "love you" lingered in an awkward place.

A place where anything I did next made me an asshole.

"I'm kidding," I blurted. "I was just fucking around."

"What?"

"I wanted to ask you to dinner tonight. Not. A date."

I cringed from my toes up. That was unexpected.

"Wow," he sounded...relieved? "You are a beast."

From Shep, that was a sign of affection.

I kept it rolling forward.

"But, will you come to dinner tonight? My mom, this is crazy, but my mom has a date."

"Good for her."

"And she wants us to come and double to make it -- easier."

"For who?"

"That's what I said! For her. And incredibly weird for everyone else. So can you go? Please? She's buying."

"What time should I pick you up?"

Shep got to my house ready to complain.

"There's not going to be any parking down there," he started. "And if there is, it's probably a long walk."

"Tonight," I warned. "You get two complaints. All night, that's it. One, two."

"Two more?"

"Yeah, two more. And once you run out you have to buy them and they cost seven dollars each. All proceeds go to me. Cash only."

Shep reflected in that moment.

"Am I a negative person?"

"I mean. You don't bring me down. But you used to have a more pleasant outlook on things."

While I was at it, I guess I did, too. Maybe it was aging. Maybe that was just the way of things.

I didn't share that.

"Let's just have fun," I did say.

"Yes. I'm having fun tonight," Shep claimed. "Whether we find parking or not."

Well, there was no fucking parking.

We ended up paying ten bucks to park in a lot a quarter mile away.

Shepherd was good to keep his face red but his complaints nil.

"This isn't a complaint: but this is why I boycott downtown."

"It wouldn't be a big deal if it were summer."

"Yeah, but it's not."

He had me there. We both sped up a little, realizing just how cold we were.

That section of town was called the Old Market. A historic area trendy with condos built into century-old, brick buildings.

The ones that were still standing. Like most parts of interesting

America, it was gentrifying. It started with one parking lot. Then came a chain drugstore.

Then the rest of the white devils converged, in business suits and tech careers. Before you knew it, half the city's history was bulldozed for a sprawling Fortune 500 campus. Layers of my childhood peeled away for consumerism and sold for profit.

It was easy to notice when you didn't live there anymore.

Everything changed between visits.

The Old Market was still hanging on to parts of its charm. Still a place you brought out-of-state relatives or gathered with friends on a hot night. But, when the Pepperjax moved in, a little soul moved out.

"It's so weird for your mom to be dating. Have you met this guy?"

"Just once, under odd circumstances. He was very handsome and very nice."

"Hmm," Shep took a sip of his beer, standing at the restaurant bar, waiting for Kim and Laith.

It was a busy restaurant. An Omaha staple.

The go-to for an impressive first date, a birthday party, a girls' night.

Black wood. White brick. White lights. Servers in long aprons.

Bartenders who knew how to make a drink.

Shep was drinking a Bud Light Lime on ice, with extra lime.

I was having a ginger ale in which I sneaked a shooter of vodka.

Just one.

These drinks: us personified.

"I don't feel like meeting anyone new," he leaned over to say. "Dating-wise."

"Me fucking either. No new niggas."

"That is uncomfortable," Shepherd squirmed.

"That's because it's not for you, and it's good for you to

remember that."

Shepherd rolled his eyes and looked around the room. Elbows up on the bar behind him. Plaid button-up. Khakis. Fleece vest.

He was dressed up.

"You look good," I complimented.

"Yeah? Thanks." He took a long pause. "You look good, too."

An afterthought.

"I thought you weren't going to say it back!"

"No -- I -- I was, but I -- I don't know. I'm an idiot."

"I was like -- damn," I played up.

"You look good. Really good. You always do. You haven't changed."

"I know -- I know. I'm actually better now."

I caught myself flirting.

"You are."

We spent a moment looking at each other.

That moment melted into smiles.

Smiles melted into goofy faces.

It all melted down into awkwardness.

What were we doing?

Shep changed the subject, shifting his body.

"So Stassi mentioned something happened between you guys? You stole her thunder or something?"

His shoulders shrugged. He pretended he was less interested than he was.

"That's not what happened."

"She said you threw yourself at some strangers."

"Have you ever seen me throw myself at anyone that wasn't an available man?"

"Uh, no."

"So, why are you entertaining her?"

"I just wanted to see what you thought. It sounded far-fetched, but…"

"Well, it's ridiculous."

"Okay. Dropped."

If I had to listen to any more of Stassi, I'd have exploded.

I'd have expended countless bits of precious energy exploding.

There was a small bit of me that would rather be talking more about us. Me and Shep.

Mom showed up in that moment, snatching that dream.

"Hi, kids," she kissed us both on the cheek, sliding between us.

I turned to greet her. Laith stood behind her as tall as a post.

"Mom, you look gorgeous," I whispered in her ear.

"Thank you, baby. This isn't alcohol, is it?"

"It's ginger ale," you nosy bitch, and I reached past her to greet her date.

"It's wonderful to see you again, Jorah," he pressed his cheek to mine.

Laith was gentlemanly. He moved with ease. Grace, in a straight way.

He weaved through the endless, full tables with perfect form.

I wanted someone like him for Mom. Someone dapper and conversational.

We sat at a round table. Shep and Laith flanking me, Mom across.

"This place is exquisite. Good choice," Laith sent in my direction.

"Oh, Mom picked it. She knows all the best places in town," I put the ball in her court  She accepted it with a smile.

"Oh, I am such a foodie, what can I say?"

She looked so proud of her use of the word "foodie," she must've forgotten the Ramen she had for lunch.

"Well, the menu looks excellent," Laith looked over his glasses and into the double-sided menu.

I looked over at Shepherd, who was absentmindedly twisting his goatee.

"What looks good to you?" I asked.

"I don't know. I'm not big on much here."

Oh my fucking god.

"There is literally something for everyone on this menu."

"I know, but their burger looks weird. They don't just have a regular burger. It's a steakburger. Is that ground beef? I don't know."

Mom and Laith were talking, unaware of Shep's complaints. I leaned over to him.

"That is your second complaint of the night. Okay? Buck up."

"One more complaint tonight?"

"Yeah, so use it wisely," I warned.

"Okay," he said. "Your breath stinks."

"Hmmph," I growled.

I moved away from him with a look. He didn't know what I was going through.

I dug in my purse and grabbed an Altoid.

He was an idiot. I hoped he was happy.

My breath? Really?

Shepherd sat back with an air of satisfaction.

"So, Shepherd, how do you two know each other? I understand you've been friends a long time?"

"Yeah. Yeah, we dated in high school."

"I was Shepherd's first love," I said, to make it more interesting. "He was the best boyfriend I've ever had."

Shep looked to me with disbelief.

Forgiving his halitosis jokes, I was sincere.

"You were," I said. "I told you that at the movies."

"And it was weird then, too."

"It should just be a compliment."

"That's a beautiful thing," Laith continued. "A lot of people never get over their first love. And even more don't get to stay lifelong friends with them."

I didn't ask if these statistics were scientific.

"Well, we got over each other," Shep laughed, and I wanted to kick him. "But we will always be friends."

I softened, examining if I felt the same.

"These two were inseparable," Mom pointed at us with a glint in her eye. "They were so cute."

A motherly recollection.

Her dark skin was radiant in the candlelight. Cheekbones and wide lips lit from beneath and casting shadows in the best spots. Beautiful, youthful skin.

I looked at Laith, who was looking at her, and I thought *He has to love her already.*

He was watching her so close. Respecting every word she said.

"I think it's possible to have that kind of connection at any age. Don't you, Kim?" He was relentless in his charm. Mom giggled, nodding in agreement.

I looked at Shep, feeling invasive. Shep raised and dropped his eyebrows.

They were in their own world.

Shep and I, outside. Freezing. Looking in.

Like kids abutted to the adults' table, waiting to be acknowledged.

He twiddled his thumbs. I pushed air from one cheek to the other.

I saw Laith's olive fingers brush over Mom's caramel ones on the stem of her glass.

And, finally:

"So, Shep, what do you do?"

He broke from Mom's eyes.

"Oh, I work at the movie theater over at the mall."

"You're still there, honey?" Mom asked in a tone that suggested something must've happened in his life.

"Yup, seventeen years in April."

"What's that saying?" Laith asked. "If you love what you do, you'll never work a day in your life."

"To loving what you do," Shep lifted his glass to begin a toast. We all met him, and I was surprisingly disgruntled.

"Shep used to act in high school. He was wonderful. I always said he should have been an actor."

Shep threw me a look.

"Oh, really?" Laith raised an eyebrow.

"He had a real gift. He should have been in the movies instead of selling tickets to them. I wanted him to move to California."

"And you didn't want to pursue acting?"

"No," Shep looked at me again, incredulously. "That's a pipe dream. It's not a real career."

"Like working in a movie theater?" I spouted, rudely.

"Jorah," Mom admonished.

She looked embarrassed.

"So, Jorah, you don't approve," Laith clarified.

"I just -- always saw more. For him," I nodded my sentence off. It was one of those things you said that you thought sounded gracious, but didn't.

"Jorah never understood that I don't need her to want more from me. I can handle my own life."

"I do understand that," I said softly, wondering where that was going.

"Why is being an actor in high school better than working at a movie theater, if he's happy there?" Laith asked with no confrontation in his voice. A feat to itself with a sentence like that.

The table paused.

Everyone was waiting for an answer. From me. They were all waiting to hear what I had to say about all the things I had to say.

I shrugged my shoulders. Looked down toward my wrapped silverware. I couldn't bear to look up.

I barely knew Laith, and he was right.

Why was I berating Shep for his chosen profession?

Had I ended up as half the things I thought I was going to be in high school?

No.

I sat like a sulking teenager for too long. No one came to save me.

"I just thought," I began. "That we would all be doing other things. And I want him to be happy," I said, again hoping to sound gracious.

"I'm happy, Jorah," Shep said. "I don't know where you've made it up that I'm not. Just because you wouldn't be happy. I'm good."

I nodded along with him, relenting.

"Okay," I said, thinking of the thousands of illegal dollars he was sitting on.

I heard a little laugh. I looked up, and Laith and Mom were swooning again. No longer interested in Shep's history.

The waitress came to take our order, and my appetite had vanished.

We rode home in near silence.

We'd gotten through the rest of dinner using random questions like you did when you first met someone.

Or when you were catching up.

We'd gotten through it with drawn-out mastication. Lingering sips of water. Cleared throats.

I couldn't read Shep anymore.

I didn't know if he was mad or disappointed. Annoyed, most definitely.

We left Mom and Laith lost in each other's eyes, waving us off.

Shep helped me put my coat on.

His cologne lasted all night.

"Are you mad?" I asked, refusing to leave the car.

"No, I'm not mad. Am I ever mad?"

"No, but I think it's because you don't process your true

emotions, not because you don't ever feel it."

"Please stop analyzing me."

I faced forward again. That didn't break down the walls I thought it would.

"I'm sorry if anything I said offended you. I don't know if I'm not communicating effectively or if I'm an asshole."

He lifted his eyebrows quickly and then let them go.

"I have a bad habit of trying to outlive everyone, Shep. I'm just now seeing it."

"It's not a competition, Jorah."

"I wouldn't win it, anyway."

"You don't need to tell your mom's new boyfriend that Shep didn't live up to his potential. You know? I guess I am kind of mad."

"I wasn't trying to be a douche," I said half-heartedly. "I was trying to care."

"That's a bad start."

"I'm really sorry."

I put my tan hand on his pink one, atop the gearshift. I rubbed the hairs on it, just to let him know. I meant it.

My hand was much softer than his.

"It's okay," he said.

I leaned over the wide expanse between us, hoping to make it look smooth.

I leaned into his face and kissed him on the mouth.

His lips were still and malleable.

And then they were reciprocal.

# 20
## The List

I WASN'T SNOOPING.

I didn't mean to find it.

I was searching for old VHS tapes. I wanted something tangible to prove that Shep was more than just another ticket checker. Another felon, waiting to be caught.

Although he asked me, in no uncertain terms, to drop it.

I didn't know how. I meant, I didn't want to.

That kiss...last night. Made me rethink everything. It was a long time coming. It was the natural way of things.

I relived every beloved moment between us. A flash of supernatural nostalgia: the beginning to the end, in a white-hot second of intimacy.

I remembered what falling in love with him felt like.  And I couldn't let myself feel that way about someone who wasn't something.

I needed him to be bigger, so I could let myself love him. That had always been the case. Lack of drive -- lack of love.

So I started searching for the tapes.

As if he'd see them and it would reignite a passion that was long dead. A drive that had never developed.

As if he'd throw off his work polo, kiss me in gratitude, and launch into some spectacular career.

I shook my head as I dug through boxes. *All the ways I can make things about me.*

I started the search for VHS tapes and ended up with my mother's bucket list instead.

Underneath her bedroom TV, where books, DVDs, and VHSs went to die, I pushed one of the baskets back into place. From underneath it poked a piece of ripped, lined paper. I grabbed the edge and pulled.

It was neatly folded, with the left side still attached to the perforation. How did she not pull that off?

I opened it carefully, like a relic, and read the contents. It was dated 11/18/14. That was the day --

That was the day I called my mother and told her about me. One of those days that was burned into your brain. The personal 9/11. What you were wearing, what you ate, what time you left the house.

You just didn't forget.

All my Shep contemplations dissolved. What did it even matter? What a waste of thought-space. Time.

The anniversary approaching faster than any other I'd ever remembered.

I read in her semi-sloppy handwriting scrawled along the top:

*Bucket List.*

And right underneath it:

*This is a list of things you do before you die.*

*(Or kick the bucket)*

Oh, she was so cute.

I instantly felt intrusive. I shouldn't have been reading that.

But there was no way I could fold it up. Pretend I hadn't seen it.

The list was written on every other line and shorter than most I had read before.

I strangely had read a lot of bucket lists. You know, zip lining, learning French, zorbing, cliff jumping...all that crazy, risk-your-life shit people did at twenty or eighty and rarely in between.

Alex and I hosted a party two years ago. Friends came over and wrote their lists down on giant sheets of paper in marker. We all shared and edited them until they were perfect. We watched videos of the most obscure items.

I checked three from mine. Three of forty.

I snatched it off my wall long ago, depressed with my progress.

I wondered if Mom felt the same way, hers tucked underneath a box, folded in pieces.

*learn to snorkel*
*go to Australia*
*take t'ai chi*
*paint and organize my basement*
*see every Elvis movie (maybe complete?)*
*see the ocean already*
*try to fall in love again*
*try to understand life*
*tell Jorah I love her every day*
*find a cure for cancer*
*don't hate God*

I sat back with the paper in my shaking hands.

Everything else grew so small.

That was before she understood what was happening to me.

Before I understood it myself.

There was no cure. If there was, it was years and billions of dollars away from us. But that didn't matter.

She accomplished quite a few of these.
And she told me she loved me every day.

# 21

## Counting Crows and Everything Else

The night before I left for Omaha was unwieldy. We abandoned work to pack my things.

Alex, reticent, made dinner in the kitchen.

No music played. Usually, there was music playing. Soul or something. Jazz.

We would have been drinking and dancing and singing and hugging.

It already felt like a goodbye. A funeral of our lifestyles.

I hated the fucking silence. I was trying to stay strong. Committed to the plan. I rolled my clothes into perfect, little tube shapes.

I pretended we weren't terrified. Devastated. Co-dependent.

My hands were shaking with nerves.

The quiet: insufferable.

That was not how we were going to say goodbye to that part of our lives. How ill-fitting. Grossly, rawly wrong.

I left my bedroom in socked feet and padded down the hall to the living room.

I could hear Alex chopping away at vegetables. He was all power and no finesse with his knife. Every medallion of carrot came with a thud of the blade to the board.

We had a state-of-the-art sound system. We were the kind of people that spent money on that stuff. It made our lives better. Loud music with pristine speakers in the walls of the rooms. You could choose to tune in or tune out.

I sat cross-legged and flipped through our rings of CDs. We had modern technology but cherished our 90s habits. Cover art and books of lyrics stashed into plastic squares in fabric binders. Counting Crows. We needed Counting Crows. *August and Everything After.* God, we needed it bad.

I slipped the disc into the CD player. Ten-disc changer, ooh la la. I flipped up the volume, filling the house with sweet and actual rock and roll.

I didn't trust people who didn't love "Round Here." There was something for everyone in that song.

I was anxious as I slipped into the doorway of the kitchen.

"Hey."

"Hey. Good choice," he referred to the music.

He didn't stop to look at me. Just kept his head down, shuttling things from the countertop to boiling water.

"Oh yeah," I said. "Can I help with anything?"

"No. You should be packing."

"I'm so fucking done with that."

"Did you get all of your shoes?"

"Just the practical ones," I said. He gave half a laugh and kept moving.

"You want a shot?"

"What? No, fuck no. You're not supposed to be drinking."

"I thought one wouldn't hurt any."

"Absolutely not."

"Okay, okay."

If I could have animated that scene there would have been four of him buzzing around the kitchen. They would have all worn the same serious look, a borderline scowl. Avoiding all contact with the one me in the door frame.

I was uncertain where to go from there.

Adam Duritz's voice blared with the emotion I couldn't release.

"Hey," I started, low.

I cleared my throat and stepped into his actual workspace.

"Hey," I tugged on his shirt, forcing him to pause. His shoulders slumped, and he inhaled deeply. He turned around.

"Hey," I repeated, with no follow-up. I was comfortable there. My tongue and ears didn't mind the sound.

"Hey" hung there, swinging back and forth between us. It didn't need anything else. It was good alone: a breath escaping my solar plexus and echoing through my mouth. Almost like not speaking at all.

"Hey," I pulled his body in with his jeans. I pressed my forehead into his chest and said it again somewhere in my silent throat.

His heart beat like a scratching dog leg. That fast repetition.

He held me at the back of the neck. Kissed the top of my hairline and farther back. I locked my arms around his waist. We were swinging back and forth, holding steady.

"Omaha" started. Like a dagger, a sharp, cold reminder of what was happening tomorrow.

Alex pulled his nose out of my curls. His face wet. Grip tight. He moved down the natural curve of my cheekbone and I moved, too. God. To touch our faces, to be so disastrously close. The sides of our mouths touched, but barely. Kissed, but only a little, before we pulled away.

Our arms wilted to our sides and our fingers found each other's and entwined. Palms touching.

I was acutely aware of my body. Of the existence of Alex. I nuzzled down between his neck and shoulder. Nose brushing.

Eyelashes on skin.
He pulled back and looked at me. Close and forward, in the eye. Back and forth so we could see all at once. Barely capturing the glances.
Alex's eyes were gray like a wolf, like a feather, like a sky. Surrounded by dark lashes.
Unkempt, dark brows. They followed the line that became his strong-bridged and narrow nose. Paved the way for solid cheekbones to turn into face. They distracted from the sweet dip of his top lip and the fullness of his bottom one -- all framed by his beard.
His old beard. Old-before-it-was-a-thing beard. The dimple in his cheek still visible and prominent through it.
That face, all mine. That smile, which I helped shape time and time again.
He was studying me, too. My almond-shaped eyes with golden middles, like wheat, like neon, like mustard. Same black eyeliner as ever, and mascara.
My thin-to-flat nose, my honey, biracial skin, my full, flesh mouth with big teeth and the beauty mark above it. High cheekbones with rounded apples if I smiled and gaunt lines if I didn't.
Long face. Longing face.
Black, unwashed curls bouncing from the top down, scalloped at the edges.
He stared. He looked right through me. A beam of holy light through his eyes and out my chest. Penetrating for miles in and around everything I'd ever been, known, or done. A part of that gigantic, messy mistake my body had made. He was a permanent structure in the architecture of my being.
It started there -- in his eyes. He kissed me. I kissed him.
The pressure was intense. Satisfying and delectable. Our hands fell into place around each other -- so close -- so close that every part of us met from the nose to the heart to the groin to the ankle.

His body felt like my body. The other half of everything.
We kissed for two songs, there like that. My stocking feet on their toes, reaching to taste and devour. More, if he'd let me.
That was so alarmingly right, I cursed time for disappearing. For taking so long. The years of our friendship, our egos, our fears, crowding out an inevitable indulgence between us.
What was meant to be.
I hated him -- but too little to stop. I hated myself. Shoving the possibility of us aside, again and again.
So many years wasted, in love with the wrong people. In bed with the wrong people.
Scared to ruin each other, the way we ruined ourselves. Scared to love. Scared to be the first to break. Scared to hurt.
We had broken each other's hearts, even so. We never tried. And here we were, too late.

We pulled away, shaking. We were both crying, and he held onto my face so tight.
So tight. Like if he never let go he could keep me forever. I reached up and held his wrists there, both of them on either side.
"Jorah," he said, gruffly, with gritted teeth.
Tears overwhelmed my face and pooled onto our feet.
"Don't say it, Alex. Don't say it."
Of course, he had said it many, many times. Nearly every day, but I knew if it escaped his lips right now, it would take a different shape. Have a different meaning.
We weren't prepared for that. It was too late for that.
"Don't say it," I begged again.
He pulled me into him and kissed my head firmly. He turned me around until he was behind me, hugging me from there, feeling my breasts as he went by.
We both worked to get my pants unbuckled to my panties underneath, our lips finding their way back to each other.

That night was just for us. Sacredly so. I felt the most alive I had felt in months. Heart beating, blood pumping, invincibly so.

I often thought about Alex's life after me. If in the free space I once occupied he'd find want for a relationship. A wife maybe. How he'd ever explain who I was. And how it wouldn't matter. I imagined she'd be jealous when I came up, so he hid me away in a cute little room in his heart. One that looked like our house and sounded like my favorite songs. His rich history well edited with me gone. He saved the good stuff for my little room and repeated it there, hearing my laugh through the course of space and time and life and what came after.

"Hello," he answered the phone on the fourth ring. The first time in days since we'd been playing hide and seek with each other. I knew he was bracing himself for the day he couldn't pick up the phone and hear me. I knew that game like I invented it. But you couldn't play like that forever.

"Hi," I said back.

*Alice: "How long is forever?"*
*White Rabbit: "Sometimes it's just one second."*

# 22
## Nebraska Nice

There was a new slogan in my home state.

It was pretty controversial when it was inducted, I heard about it all the way in Texas.

*Nebraska Nice.*

Very exciting. As though people didn't already have a hard time knowing where Nebraska was on the map. The least they could do was give you a reason to want to.

It wasn't that it wasn't true.

People in Nebraska were...nice.

Midwesterners as a whole, I supposed, were known for their agreeable nature. And their lack of accents. The heartland.

I thought the word "nice" was one of the worst adjectives on the planet. Odd, fun, abrasive, creative, generous, honest, compassionate. All words you could use to get to the heart of a person. Nice, by comparison, was very surface. It was not a real quantifier of character.

People in Nebraska did nice things.
That didn't mean they were nice people.
You bumped into someone at the grocery store, you both smiled and apologized. You gave someone directions and maybe even drove ahead, signaling their turn. You took the extra time to talk to your mailman, wave to your neighbor, engage with your waitress.
All very, very nice things. Very polite. Very Nebraska.

But, those human GPSs. Those apologizing, door-holding, sweethearts didn't actually give a shit about other people.
It was in the way they voted. The way they commented on news stories. That was Nebraska Nice. Passive-aggression. Judgmental eyes. False smiles. Lying to make it sound good.
But they'd help you move in the rain.
I was at war with it. I wanted more truth, depth, sincerity -- out of everything.
Squeezing the juice from the plum until my hand was raw.
Demanding more from people than they were able to give.
It wasn't until I left that I understood how mean nice could actually be.

So I couldn't say I was surprised when I sneaked off to Stassi's parents' restroom and heard the conversation turn to me.

I had known Stassi's family as long as I had known her.
Sleepovers. Dinners. Tubing trips. Musicals.
I spent many nights with the Whitakers, considering myself part of them. Not because I needed a social adoption but because they insisted I was. So I was.
Stassi's family was the epitome of the mid-western all-American dream. The sweet-voiced mother with a kind heart. The tough dad who loved football and grilled a mean steak. Three blonde

girls, with varying degrees of accomplishment and looks. The white Kardashians, they liked to think. I loved her parents and often sought her mother for advice. As Stassi did mine. I had the crazy idea I was free to be myself around them. Yes, I was different, but valid.

When I would come visit, the conversations would begin with innocent questions. Asking about my life, catching up with what I had been up to and then a remark would come from the left:

*Have you seen that Rihanna video about drugs? It reminded me so much of you.*

Or a question:

*So, dancing on tables, naked, really?*

Accompanied by a disapproving look -- and a perplexed me. It took me a while to catch on. I would play it off as though they were joking, but they weren't joking. They were shaming me. The way Nebraskans shame. With a smile on their face and a judgment behind their eye. And a complete forgiveness of their own wild ways. It was so subtle and well practiced, you didn't know how to react other than to go with it. Whether the stories were true, or grossly exaggerated or completely fabricated didn't matter. Their minds were made up. And you didn't rock the boat, so you just let it slide.

It was one of those things you couldn't prove in court. You could explain it to someone but it was so below the surface you would have had to get yourself dirty, so you didn't. I thought maybe I was making it up, maybe I was sensitive. But then it became a recurring thing. A trolling. I wanted some other adjectives from Nebraska Nice, and I got them from the people I loved and trusted. Judgmental, invasive, hypocritical, underhanded. I suspected that mostly stemmed from Stassi's narration. Things that made me sound bad to make her look better.

I got it. Nebraska Nice.

I was surprised Stassi contacted me at all.
The ride home, and the days after SpiritCycle, were full of tension. Well, silence. We hadn't spoken. I gave her time and space. Not expecting that she would have seen my side, but that we would have let it settle and moved on -- the way we always had. Me, sucking it up. Her, pretending it never happened.

*My parents want you and Shep over for dinner tonight if you're free.* She texted.

*Okay. Is that cool with you?*

*Yeah, it'd be fun. They'd love to see you.*

I thought for a while before I replied, considering the night. Me, blending in, the way they liked me to. Subconsciously fighting the stigmas imposed on me.
Quieter. Non-controversial. Watered-down cocktail.
Turtleneck and jeans instead of a v-neck and mini skirt.
The way you dimmed and dumbed yourself, when you knew you were the topic of conversation the moment you left the room.

*Sure, I'll be there.*

A willing participant in my own dissipation. That could be the last time I saw those people. Who would I be?

"Oh, hi! I love that look on you," Stassi's mom's soft-spoken voice met me at the door with a big hug.

"Hello, Mrs. Whitaker."

"Oh stop, you can call me Jan now."

"I couldn't." The formalities of our original relationship were more comfortable to me than first names. I smiled tightly and loosened the collar around my Nebraska Huskers turtleneck.
Stassi's middle sister, DeAnna, was sprawled over the sofa. A coal mine of eyeliner. White blonde hair growing out hard at the top. Stomach pouring from under a too-short shirt. One of her children's fathers next to her, belching.

"Sup, slut?" she said.

"Hey," I waved my hand in a circular motion, not wanting to engage. DeAnna and I had our fair share of confrontations -- mostly orchestrated through her sister.

You could be wondering why I kept Stassi's friendship so long if that was the way I felt about it. Look at your friend's list, you have a Stassi, too. And if you don't? Well, good for fucking you.

"Shep will be here soon. You want a drink? Wine?"

"She wants a shot," DeAnna said, pulling her shirt over her stomach.

"I'll just have a water, thanks."

"You okay, baby?" Stassi asked with concern.

"I'm fine. Just taking it easy."

Stassi disappeared around the corner into the kitchen.

"You know my fiancé, Ricky," DeAnna said.

"Hi, Ricky," I reached over to shake his hand.

Ricky was at least in his early forties. Covered in tattoos. And smelled like cocaine from where I was standing. All things I couldn't have cared less about, all things I'd heard the Whitakers denounce throughout the years. Especially the evils of ink.

"Hey," he met my handshake. "Nebraska fucking sucks." He pointed at my shirt.

"Actually, it's really nice."

Around the dinner table, my anxiety lessened. Shep sat next to me; there was a playful vibe between us. Mr. Whitaker had made his Omaha-famous ribs.

Stassi kept offering me alcohol. Maybe I should have replayed her concerned voicemail to her. Alcohol and aging.

"So, Jorah, what brings you back home?" Mrs. Whitaker asked between bites. The beating heart of their family.

"I missed my mom," I half fibbed.

I couldn't keep up with all the reasons I gave people.

"I'm sure she loves having you back."

"I love being back. You spend so many years away it's hard to remember what's home and what's not."

"That's why I like my girls right here. They always know where home is. It's dangerous out there. It's so easy to lose your way when you don't have strong roots."

Stassi and DeAnna nodded in smug agreement. Smug, never-left-the-state, agreement.

"Well, I think my roots are pretty strong. Some branches just need a wider space to grow." What were we talking about? Trees? Or -- or what here?

I shifted uncomfortably in my body and thoughts.

*Stassi dropped LSD in her living room.*

*DeAnna just got out of a three-month coke binge.*

"So what's your job down there, again?" DeAnna pointed at me with her fork. "Stassi said you were running a photo booth thing, right? For, like, children's parties."

"Photo booth thing," I repeated under my breath.

I looked at Stassi, who wasn't looking at me.

"I own a photography studio. With my partner. Alex. It's a little more involved than that." I was angry at my voice for wobbling in consternation.

Shep looked over at me and stuck his tongue out. He grabbed my kneecap. Maybe he could read my thoughts.

*If you can read my thoughts, squeeze my knee again.*

He squeezed. Whoa.

"Weren't you guys listed in a *Forbes* article?" Shep bumped my shoulder with his shoulder.

"Yes! We were. Thank you." *Wedding Day. Forbes.* Same thing. Photo booth thing.

"But weren't you doing a sexy maid service thing? Where you show up and clean a stranger's house in your panties? You're so crazy." DeAnna snickered.

"Uh, yes," I cleared my throat. "That was my job about nine years ago. And I loved it. I thought we talked about this then."
DeAnna made an incredulous face. Eyes bugged. Mouth turned down.

"Wasn't that the same year you worked for UNICEF?" Shep barged in again.

"It was. That's how I afforded travel," I smiled up at him. I wanted to kiss him.

"What's that? Unicef. Sounds like a cold medicine," Ricky asked.

"It's a world-wide charity organization," I spouted, without further detail.

"Well, I didn't know you did that. Good. Good for you," Mr. Whitaker nodded in approval.

"Thank you. I spent three months in a jungle, so I'd think you'd have heard of that."

"Oh, you saw all those skinny kids, with flies on their faces or some shit? Did you ever want to get one and give it a home?" Ricky kept talking. "I always thought if I got one, I'd give it a home, no matter how dirty or messed-up they were. I sent in money once to Boys Town, or whatever. Save the Children. Ten cents a month -- it's a like a million dollars over there."

The table ate.

"So. Alex?" Mrs. Whitaker started. "You said partner. Is he your boyfriend, then?"

Shep scooted uncomfortably in his seat.

"Alex is..." I felt a prickly protectiveness. "Alex is my business partner and best friend."

"But not your boyfriend?"

"No."

I almost laughed at how trivial the word boyfriend was compared to the magnitude of our relationship.

"Isn't he gay?" DeAnna loudly asked, squinting her eyes like she didn't understand her own question.

"No," I chortled.

"Yes, he is. Stassi told us this really funny story. About Alex pretending to be gay to get you guys out of some crazy situation. Something about a drug bust. What was that Stassi?"

I quickly flipped through all my Alex stories. The two times they'd met. It didn't take long to realize that it never happened.

"I don't remember that story, Stassi," I turned to her. "Why don't you tell it again?"

Stassi sipped her diet pop through a straw, avoiding eye contact. We'd gone the entire meal without so much as exchanging a smile. My arms were going numb: a tell-tale sign of my fleeting patience. I excused myself from the table and into the adjacent restroom. I paced the small square footage. Was that what she brought me here for?

How did she dare bring up Alex? Alex was sacred. She didn't just get to talk about him with her family -- with anyone. He wasn't hers to discuss.

I heard Alex's name in the next room. I stopped pacing to listen. It was Shep.

"Alex is a great guy. I've hung out with him a few times. He's been around forever. I can't believe you guys haven't met him."

"I don't know. He's always given me a weird vibe. He's feminine to me. I don't like guys that wear tank tops. And she says they're doing really well, but..." Stassi's voice became quiet.

It was followed by a collective gasp and an "Oh no."

"Stassi," Shep started, half dismissively.

"Is that why she's really back?" DeAnna asked. "You know it's not for her mom, you said she treats her mom like shit."

"I don't know," Stassi said. "Maybe she's pregnant."

"She's not pregnant," Shep interjected.

"She's probably pulling a Jorah and running away from all responsibility, looking for a free ride," DeAnna said.

"Is that what that's called, 'pulling a Jorah'?" Mrs. Whitaker asked, amused.

"In this family, yes." They all started to laugh.

"Did she ever pay you back for your bridesmaid dress, Stassi?"

"Not as of today. My fourth anniversary just passed. I think she needs to clean a few more houses in her underwear," Stassi snorted.

They all shushed each other, getting ready to smile in my face upon my return.

Nebraska Nice.

I looked in the mirror. That stupid turtleneck. That stupid headband. How could words make me feel so small? Like a speck of dust. I didn't remember a time I felt like that.

I exhaled a few times. I didn't recognize the girl breathing back at me. I didn't wear my hair like that. I didn't line my lips like that. I hated things that constricted my neck, and I always wore black eyeliner. Always. The girl in the mirror was a fabrication. A lie, just like they wanted.

They were my people. I thought they were. I thought I belonged to them. How could they share such callous disregard for who I was? Where did that start? They had no idea -- all the things I'd gone through. How far I'd come. Writhing, painful, sweaty nights -- losses and gains and losses again.

Those weren't my people, I recalibrated. I belonged solely to myself. I breathed deeper. Eyes closed, wishing I could flush myself down the toilet and back to somewhere safe. Back to my mother. My mother and her "weak roots."

A tree they thought could be so easily tipped over. A tree that withstood losing men and mothers and a child. My mother raised me to be kind. Not nice. My Josephine, my Ursula...my roots. Stassi had picked fruit from that true and still denied its existence. Because regardless of how she was for others, she was that for me. My Josephine. My roots.

My roots went so fucking deep and wrapped around the core of the earth and burst back through my mind like a supernova. They burned bright and tangled, enraptured in everything I touched and did. My roots were a gift from a woman who had spent her life digging deeper into the soil of truly living just to help me plant them. They were six feet deep and then on like that forever. So deep god didn't have an ax big enough to tear that tree down. Stassi had poisoned everything I loved about myself. Exploited my insecurities. Downplayed my triumphs. My experience with life, fodder for family dinner. Gossip. Things you raised eyebrows at.
Something crazy stirred in me.
A composite of all those bits of me.
A pure fury built from pain. From the necessity to be understood -- from the waste of eighteen years with a person who never knew how to love me. From my foolishness of thinking it was ever something different.
The something crazy won.

The bathroom door squeaked open.
A moment of silence as they scrambled for a new topic. I closed my eyes. *Something crazy won.* I put one foot in front of the other until I was standing in the dining room. Clothes in hand. Entirely nude.
The parents jumped up. The rest of them gasped. But I didn't really see them. I was somewhere else. I was burying my roots through their house. So they'd never forget.

"I have nothing to hide," I told them, probably out loud. "If you want to throw stones, do it now. So I can see the bruises. I don't clean in my underwear anymore, but I was really fucking good at it."

I pulled my underwear from my clothes and threw them onto the table. They wrapped over the meat.

"You can have them."

Shep jumped up to shield me, and he pushed me toward the front door. The family erupted into angry words I didn't make out.

"Is she crazy?" I heard that one. I left it in the house behind me.

It was freezing outside, and I was in the world naked. SpiritCycle be damned; that was close to Zen.

I ran off their property and around a retaining wall. I threw my clothes to the ground. Hands on my knees, hunched over, cow back.

I was laughing hysterically. I was crying. I was free.

I heard the screen door slam shut, and Shepherd and Stassi barreled out of the house. I grabbed my pants to pull them back on. They found me, one leg in.

"Oh god, she's still naked," Shep turned his back to me.

"What the hell was that, Jorah? You're, like, banned now from my house."

I kept laughing.

"This is the worst thing you've ever done! What is wrong with you?"

"Stassi," I said, through tears. "Fuuuuuuck you, okay? And everyone in that house." I flipped her two birds. I kissed them and flipped them again.

"You guys need something to talk about so badly, this should last a lifetime."

"What are you talking about? What is she talking about?" Stassi maintained her innocence.

Somewhere a star exploded inside my mind.

I came closer to her. Jeans on. Tits out. No cares.

"I hate who you are."

I was heaving. Out of breath and to the brim with anger.

Shep kept his head down. Stassi stood there, on the verge of tears, defensive and speechless.

And there we all were. The three of us. Just as we had been, sharing space hundreds of times before. Our chests pumping hard in varying degrees of emotion. The innocence of our surface relationships completely shattered.

"I don't feel sorry for you," I continued. Something in my voice sounded like someone else. "I don't deserve that. You liar."

"I'm going to get you home," Shep took me by the shoulders.

"You scare me Jorah. You're unstable," Stassi spat behind me. "I've never said anything that wasn't true! You're crazy."

I leaped out of Shepherd's grasp and pointed my finger in her face. Teeth bared. Feral, as broad as the moon. I could swallow her up.

"YOU deserve the short life." I spewed at her feet. Shep grabbed me again around the waist and peeled me off into his car. "I hope you die!"

"Don't you ever come around my family again!" Stassi disappeared into the house.

I fell to pieces in the passenger seat.

"I know what you're going to say."

Shep's car was parked in my driveway, still running. The drive home was infused with my sobs and laughs. An unbearable symphony. He rubbed my back, staring at the road.

"You do?"

"I know you think I'm a wild animal. I came home and started tearing things apart."

"I don't think that."

"I just went there for food! I didn't know this was going to happen."

"I'm glad you stood up for yourself. I didn't like the things they were saying."

"I heard them in the bathroom and I just -- I snapped."

"No, you stripped."

"I stripped. I was trying to make a point."

"I think you made one."

"Stassi's never going to talk to me again."

"It didn't sound like you cared about that."

"I lost my shit because I do care, Shep! I care too much."

"I know you do."

"That wasn't me talking," I whispered. He glossed over it. That could all have been so much easier if I had just told them the truth. I didn't. Not then.

"I don't think she'll ever self-reflect. See where I'm coming from," I sighed.

"Maybe not. But she saw a nipple. And a nipple goes a long way."

Shep made me laugh, so easily. Like he did.

"Stassi has her flaws. As we all do. But I don't think she actually means any harm."

"Oh god, please don't do that. Please don't stand up for her. You heard the shit she said. I may be pregnant? Like. I can't -- just please don't stand up for her. You know that shit is wrong."

"I'm not! I'm not trying to."

"It sounds like you're saying it's okay for her to be a dick, because she's also dumb," I pouted.

Shep sighed. He looked at me with his head relaxed on the seat. He moved a stray curl out of my face. I felt close with him. The anxiety lifted a little.

"You shouldn't have told her she deserves to die young."

"No, god, no. I shouldn't have."

"Jorah, you -- you've been told your whole life, you're someone special. You're someone unique. You know? You get whatever you want, you do things differently. And there's just nobody like you.

And that's hard for Stassi. You are rare. And Stassi would rather dim that then celebrate that. And she definitely can't admit it." Most things Shep said filtered through my mind and out again. But one thing stuck. Like sticky, beautiful glue.

"You think I'm rare?" my voice barely escaped.

"Yes, I do. Of course I do."

# 23

## Roxy

I had this friend back in Austin. Years ago. And for a while, we were known as salt and pepper. We were both brown so I didn't know which was which. I supposed it depended on who was looking. Her name was Roxy. Her real name was Thai, and she refused to share it with anyone. Roxy and I would go out and tag-team the town after work most nights, either with a group or just the two of us. I appreciated Roxy for many things. Her insane ability to go out all night and never spend a dime, her relentless empathy, and her "bomb-ass kitchen skillz."

One night, Roxy and I had plans to go out. Alex had recently broken up with one of the other waitresses, subsequently quit the bar, and was desperate for me to help him grieve and bitch.

"Just come out with us."

"No way. She's friends with Rox and I just don't want to hear it."

"Okay. I'll come home." Co-dependence did what it was begged

to do.
I broke the news to Roxy and, in her usual way, she went on with life.

"That's cool, go be with that asshole," she said with a long, red smile and her teeth and eyes glistening.

"I know," I rolled my head back with exaggerated ire. "Shots?"
I stayed at the bar for an extra hour pre-gaming my shit talking with shit talking. Leaning too far over the bar, screaming at our bartender, whispering fake secrets. I left eventually to go be with Alex, and Roxy continued her plans for the night.

"Brunch tomorrow."

"For sure, beotch. Love you."
Kisses. Kisses. Goodbye.

They found her the next morning, car wrapped around a tree. Her body flung through the windshield, lifeless -- mixed in the dirt and brush.

We closed the bar that day: an incredible feat for our income-obsessed owner. We all met there, in various stages of grief and disbelief. Blaming ourselves or mad at Roxy. Bawling into each other's shoulders or playing her songs loud on the jukebox. Seth, the bartender who served her was the most visibly devastated. He pounded his fist into the bar and screamed. He threw shot glasses. He hid his face in his broad hands.

"I didn't know," he kept reassuring everyone. "I didn't know she was fucked-up like that. It wasn't a crazy night." Seth had been drinking, too; we all had. There was no way to know.
I sat in a booth. Legs curled to my chest, head down, holding court as everyone came to check on me. I didn't want to be seen, but I didn't want to be alone. I wanted to talk to Roxy. I wanted to rewind everything back to last night and meet up with her after all. I knew I could've stopped this if I had been with her. But maybe,

I just would've been there, too. Maybe my judgment would have been no better than hers.

Roxy wanted to own a restaurant. A Thai restaurant using her family's recipes. She talked about what it would have meant to her grandmother that she honored their traditions that way. That she hadn't lost her roots in the Western world.

"I'm going to name it *Sasithorn*, just for her. That's her name, and all the food is hers so it's fitting, right? I mean, these white mouths aren't going to know what hit them, honestly. I want the whole place to be an experience. Like you come in and, boom, you're in Thailand. In the jungle or on the beach; I haven't decided. Everyone on the floor -- on carpets and pillows. I want the food made just for you, in front of you. Does that sound badass? Here have some more rice. Yes, and then pour that sauce over your rice. That's good. Thai food is like a ballet, I mean really. It's delicate, it's balanced, it's harmonious, it's intricate. It is, by far, the ONE thing I KNOW that I know. So I want to do this, and then I'm going to fly Sasithorn out here and surprise her. She will be so amazed and so proud. I just picture her little face -- beaming. Oh, and I want pictures of her on the wall. She's like the Colonel of the place. Here, have some more."

I watched Roxy cook meals for us countless times. She took time and pride and care, in every dish. That's how I was remembering her. That's how she really was.

In the bar world, it's really easy to sacrifice your true heart for popular personality. On some level, we all did it. You came here to hide, to drink, to not exist in the ways you knew you did.

The weeks following were quiet and hard. Some stayed every night to drown their pain, others snuck home post-shift. Clocking out with no goodbyes. I struggled to understand why Roxy and not me. Why Roxy and not anyone else? I wondered where her dreams went. Why should hers be cut short and anybody else's seen to fruition? I wondered if that restaurant would've ever opened anyway, and I knew the answer to that, somewhere deep. Was it all just as random as the spin of a steering wheel?

Roxy was sent home to Thailand for her funeral. She hadn't lived there since she was three, but her family wanted her on homeland. Thai funerals were beautiful events that could last days; you were cremated and mixed with flowers in the end. Something better than being six feet deep in Texas, near strangers, underfoot.

We held a fundraiser, soon after, to help her parents with the cost. Then, a memorial for friends to come and tell stories, and a release with pink and gold balloons sent into the sky. The first year we held an anniversary party; we all drank pineapple rum like she liked and told the same stories. Stories that we loved but didn't quite capture her, either. The second year, a lot of us had left. I had left. Some had moved altogether, some had children. I stopped in, and there were a few recognizable faces at the end of the bar, drinking together and being wistful.

The third year I heard from and spoke to no one. The day came and went and I forgot which day it was. Years later, I remembered this girl that I used to know that used to know me. She could have been dead, we could have lost touch. It all blended and blurred inconsequentially. What she wanted. Who she was beneath the superficial self. It didn't mean anything, really. If that was true for her, then it was true for me, too. How sad, when we were all destined to be forgotten. If we were ever known in the first place.

# 24

## Secret Wonton

I was awoken on a Tuesday by a call from Shep. I was thankful for it.

I had been having this dream about Stassi. We were back in high school, and she was spreading rumors around the halls that I didn't exist. Everyone believed her. I was yelling at familiar faces, "Hey, I'm here!" They didn't turn toward me; they kept talking and laughing. Eating lunch.

I looked down and my hands were disappearing. Blinking in and out. I clapped them together, and they'd go through each other. But I felt so real. I was thinking and walking. My legs vanished, and then I was floating. Until I looked in a mirror and there was no one there. No reflection.

Stassi walked in the bathroom I was in. And she looked just like me.

The phone ringing was a pleasant surprise. Shep's name appearing was an even greater one. I was amazed, yet again, he wasn't holding the other night over my head. I had decided that if he did, I would sit him down and tell him what was going on. But, I was so relieved not to tell him. Yet, anyway.

"Good morning," I answered.

"Hey. How are you?"

"Good. I'm sleeping in, I guess."

"I guess. It's almost noon."

"Yeah, well, I'm a night owl, you know."

"Yeah. So, what do you have going on tonight?" he cut to the chase, unexpectedly.

"I am -- well, nothing. Half the people I hang out with hate me."

"Good. You want to do something with the other half?"

"Oh!"

I checked in with myself. I was groggy. How would I feel in a few hours? I couldn't sit in a dark theater anymore this month.

"I don't want to go see a movie," I warned. "I've seen so many, my eyes can't adjust to daylight."

"No, no movie."

I perked up out of curiosity. What else would Shep be doing if it wasn't the almighty cinema?

"Okay. What are we doing?"

"It's a surprise. But I'll get you at four."

"Four! Okay -- that's, that's cool."

"Dress casual," he hung up the phone mysteriously.

Dress casual? What's casual to Shep? Does he know what's casual to me?

I had thought a lot about the kiss. It made me blush -- nervous. I kind of hoped it would happen again.

Maybe, subconsciously I took my clothes off at Stassi's in hopes of a seduction? That was stretching it.

I wasn't expecting an attraction to Shepherd. That's actually the last thing I would have thought could happen here. But, it was happening.

I didn't want it. I did, but when I looked at all the cards on the table, it wasn't a fair game to play.

I had to return this burgeoning excitement for him to its friendship shelf. Sit there. Shut up. And friend.

"Hey!"

I hopped in with Shep. I had chosen jeans, running shoes, and a t-shirt with a jacket.

"Casual?"

I flaired my arms.

"Perfect choice."

"Where are we going?"

I was giddy, and I walked my fingers up his shoulder in anticipation. That wasn't friending, that was flirting. And I pulled them back.

"Somewhere you wouldn't expect."

"Oh -- kay."

"I want to talk to you." He took a pause.

The radio was on instead of a CD, so I knew he was serious about conversation. This was it. This was where he let me have it. I knew I wasn't getting off so easily.

"You seem unhappy here."

I let that sink in, wondering if it was true. Weird: I didn't know the answer myself.

"Are you unhappy here?"

"I don't know. It's all very different."

"You've been short and angry."

"I have?"

Shep's eyes bugged. It was that obvious.

"You've also gotten naked in the Whitaker's house. I don't have to remind you."

"No. No, that's unforgettable."

"And, it's not like you. You're the one who tells ME I can't complain. Or I'm like Eeyore or something. But you --"

I stared at my hands, trying to make sense of all my actions. What did this look like from the outside?

"I'm not worried, but I am concerned. I don't like seeing this side of you. I know something's wrong."

"I think -- I'm just adjusting."

"Maybe."

"It's hard to be back and leave my life behind."

"So then why did you?"

I'd run dry of excuses. It made no sense to leave Austin, and my company and my home, to come to Omaha and be miserable. My facade was cracking.

"I don't know," I admitted.

"You've always, always, said that if you don't like something, change it."

"I was just so full of quotes for everyone's life."

"Yeah, yeah you were. Did something happen with Alex?"

"No! No."

"You keep saying he's coming here. I saw your reaction when his name was mentioned. Are you running from him?"

"What was my reaction? No, no I'm not running from Alex." I laughed off the idea.

We exited the interstate on the south side of Omaha. A place that used to be stockyards for the booming beef industry and was now left in an industrial shamble.

Maybe he was taking me to tacos. They have the best tacos down there.

"I'm not running from anything," I assured us both. "I just -- I thought it was going to be different."

"What? Omaha?"

"I don't know yet, Shep. I don't have answers."

"It's okay. I just wanted to ask. I wanted you to know that I'm here."

He put his hand on my knee and squeezed.

"Thank you," I looked at him, sullen.

"I didn't mean to bring you down. I hope this picks you up," he parallel parked in front of a small white building on a corner of a street the city had neglected.

You knew those streets when you saw them. They were in minority neighborhoods. Potholes so big you could see the hundred-year-old brick underneath. This was the Mexican part of town. A lot of streets were just like this.

"Where are we?"

"We are at the Salvation Army."

"Are we thrifting?"

"No," he got out of the car and I followed.

"We," he continued as we walked next to each other, "are volunteering."

"What do you mean?"

"I come here every month and help out in the kitchen."

"You do?"

I stopped walking and my jaw hit my sternum.

"Yeah, I do. For years now. I know that I'm shattering this perception you have of Shepherd who does nothing and doesn't even know he's alive, blah, blah, blah. So here it is."

"Shep, I never thought that," I said. What a complete lie. He was right. That was exactly who I thought he was.

I followed Shep into the building, through an aging lobby, and into a bright dining room.

Sixty tables with benches. Stainless steel ones with chafers on them. Seven older black ladies with aprons and hairnets.

"Hey, Shep," one of them said, with a wave of hip and hand.

"Hey, Ms. Tanisha," he returned, with the same inflection.

I traveled behind him, feeling shy. Shep walked up and hugged her.

"You brought me some extra hands?"

"I have. This is Jorah, she's a good friend."

"Hi, nice to meet you," I stuck out my hand and smiled. She took my one hand in both of hers.

"Thank you for coming in. We're expecting quite a few extras tonight. Do you know how to shuck corn?"

A few minutes later, after meeting the whole crew, Shep and I donned our aprons and hairnets in a back corner alone.

Well, not alone. There were 200 ears of corn with us. Perfectly ripe and ready to be slathered in butter and devoured.

"I can't believe this is where you brought me," I exclaimed.

"Do you like it?"

"I love it. I'm so excited; I just can't believe it."

"Coming here, with these ladies, always makes me feel good. So I thought it may cheer you up, too."

I couldn't help the goofy, toothy smile that came over me as I looked up at Shep. I felt taken care of.

"It does Shep. I feel really good."

"Good."

"I bet you bring all your girls here," I said, hoping it came off as a joke and not jealousy.

"Ha. No. These ladies love me, they'd get jealous. I did try to bring Stassi once. She wasn't into it."

"Yeah," I shrugged.

"And that's cool. It's not for everybody."

"How did you start working here?"

"Ms. Tanisha, she comes to see all the black movies and makes me laugh. I hook her up with popcorn. She invited me once and I came down. I didn't think it'd be a regular thing."

"This is a whole new side of you, Shep."

"No, it's an old side of me. It's new to you. I thought you'd be happy here. It's hard to be a Gremlin when you're helping people."

"Yeah."

Wait.

"Hey!" I hit Shep with the husks I was holding.

"Wait until you meet the people that come here," he shucked and talked. "They look -- well, god, I hate the word homeless."

"Really?"

"I hate it. Because, like most of these guys are vets. And the rest are single moms with their kids. So I don't like them being called 'homeless,' they're just people, you know? I mean, at any time any one of us could be them."

Shep was deconstructing his ears, expertly. His voice light, commanding. Hairnet. Plastic gloves. Apron. Shep. His sweet heart, manifested. I was seeing him for who he really was and not who I'd decided he was.

I grabbed the leaves and tassels at the top of the ear. Pulled down in one good yank. Repeated until the ear was clean. Tossed the husks away. I'd known how to do this my whole life. Second nature.

"So what next?" I bounced into the car, feeling lighter than I had all year.

"I hadn't thought that far ahead."

"I don't want to go home."

Shep chuckled to himself. "You used to say that all the time."

"When?"

"When we were kids. When we were together. You NEVER wanted to go home. You always wanted to get to the next thing."

I thought back. There were no concrete memories, but I knew it was true.

"Well, there were WAY more interesting things happening outside of my house."

"Yes, I know. You dragged me to all of them."

"Now you dragged me somewhere, and I'm not done hanging out."

I didn't really wonder if I were coming on too strong because I knew I was. Like when you felt high, but you weren't. Like you drank too much coffee, and anything could happen? Being with Shep was igniting my veins, against everything I did to put the fire out. It was more powerful. Who was I kidding? I hadn't tried to put the fire out.

"I haven't seen your place, this whole time," I told him as he started the car. "I want to see where you live."

"It's far from exciting."

"I don't care, it's yours." The words were sliding out of my mouth with so much ease I felt out-of-body.

"Okay."

He put the car in gear and drove. It was reaching sunset. That late-October cool. The blood-orange sun cast shadows, and I breathed in how beautiful Nebraska could be.

I wondered how pure the landscape would be with the removal of humans. Just...exactly what it was. No power lines and roads. I'd never been anyplace with no power lines or roads. Even the remote places I'd been, I'd taken roads to get there.

Dirt-covered ones. Gravel ones. Suggested ones. It would have felt good to find a place without one. If that existed.

If you were driving west in Omaha at sunset, the sun would blind you. It was unforgivingly bright and the hills didn't help. You needed sunglasses and a hat and shade pulled down, for those roads. It had always been that way. And it always would be.

Shep's apartment was nothing exciting. It was his teenage bedroom, expanded and with a cat, Gumper. And with less food. But it was clean. It was clean as fuck.

He had a lot of posters up. Movie posters, on every wall. I didn't know how much movie posters were worth, but I knew he had a shit ton of them and hadn't paid a dime. An expansive library of DVDs. Even some VHSs. And curtains that told me his mother had dropped by.

"I told you it was nothing special."

"Eh," I replied. "What's it supposed to be? The Taj Mahal?"

"Well, exactly. I'm barely here. You want a beer?"

I halted, second-guessing myself. "No. That's okay."

Shep pulled out one for himself and poured me a glass of iced tea. Without me asking. I smiled and thanked him. He sat across from me and there was a quiet between us. We had a million things to say, but we didn't.

Everything was fuzzy like I might not remember it all the next day, and I was trying to hold onto every moment as it came. My hands reached for the memory of his sturdy back. My legs around his hip bones. His breath staggered aside my face. He said my name slightly, and I held on to it. We didn't look at each other. I kept my eyes mostly closed. The strangeness of that room, the apartment windows, one vanilla candle. It all struck a note of my past. Surroundings that felt like those college days after I left. The cool breeze of strange. Chilly bed sheets and sweaty drunk bodies. We weren't there yet. We weren't sweaty. We were way too polite for that. More experienced now than we were before. We had learned restraint. Decorum. Shame. It showed in our polite thrusts and soft hands.

"Shep," I whispered, almost grunted.

"Yeah?"

"Choke me."

Everything stopped. Our bodies stopped. I tried to remember the steps we took to get here, but couldn't find the way back.

Something about iced tea.

Something about a strange kiss.

Something about anger.

"What's that?"

I wriggled underneath his weight.

"Choke me."

I put my hands across my own neck to show him what I was talking about. What I was asking for.

"Jorah, don't be weird. This is getting weird."

I looked at him, finally, in the eye.

I didn't flinch or shy away, because I didn't want him to.

"Just try it."

He sighed and braced himself up with one arm, using the other to place his fingers around my neck. He stroked it deeply, instead of a grasp. He just kind of hard pet it. I grabbed his hand, clasped my own on top of it, and held it there tightly.

"Like this," I pressed.

"I don't want to hurt you."

"It doesn't hurt."

He set his jaw and got into it again. We went back to no eye contact and let our bodies communicate.

The politeness made way for passion.

I felt how much we wanted each other again.

Something about history.

Something about loss.

I gave in to the black out.

The next morning, and Shep was gone.

# 25

## MAKE IT COUNT

IN THE STRANGE BED, EYES STILL CLOSED, I REACHED OVER TO FEEL his body. My own body stretched for comfort, exhausted. I'd need to sleep. I had learned to listen closer when she spoke.

My hands met more jersey sheets and the cool pillowcase next to me. A little sadness mixed with relief. Last night was a surprise, maybe it was best we didn't face the morning's questions right away. I felt a piece of paper on the pillow.

He was so cute. Just like in the movies. I picked it up and brought it to my face.

I couldn't make it out. I squeezed my eyes and opened them again. There was nothing.

The panic took a short cut. Again, I squeezed my eyes tight to make sure I was actually opening them. I was. Everything was a haze as gray as the sky had been. I could make out the light through the window and the shadow of the doorway, but it was all glossed over in fog.

"Shep? Shep?!" I called out, knowing he was gone. My body

turned to a stack of bones, a newborn fawn, an alien. Fumbling its way from the mattress to the floor, knees hobbled, hands helpless and desperate.

Full, full, full of the most bitter fear I'd ever tasted. I searched in the dark for my phone. I knew I'd left it on the nightstand by the bed. My muscles memorized the room, and my thigh hit the table. I reached out and heard it hit the ground. I hit the ground, too.

"No, no, no," I cried out, my heart breaking. Naked on my hands and knees, and my fingertips desperate over the carpet.

I needed help. It echoed in my head, the hardest words. The moment I'd been dreading since treatment. Since the last time Alex lifted my failing form from the bathtub to the bed. Since the last time my mother held me shivering, using her body to try anything to keep me warm.

I needed help.

I brushed the edge of the phone and grasped it, pulling it in. I put it right at eye level and saw the white light come on. I told it to dial Mom, and it did. The phone rang, and my body writhed in uncertainty. I sat up and put my head on the bed, eyes closed.

"Hello," my mother picked up.

I opened my mouth to speak, and I felt a loosening in my lower half, followed by an uncontrollable loss of bowel.

"Hello," my mother repeated.

I opened my mouth to speak and nothing came out but wailing.

I hated hospitals. I hated the way they smelled. The lighting overhead. I hated that you never knew what was going to happen on the other side of the doors. I hated the stench of corporate interest and prescription pills. The last time I was in an Austin hospital, I was told to check in with Omaha doctors. Their "team." One of the best in the nation.

I'd rather be dead than die the small deaths I had in chemo. But, after Shep's, I realized that small deaths were just part of the

package.
I was told this would be a "fight." I had to put up a *fight*. A fight for my life. The fight of my life.
It wasn't a fight. It was like walking blindfolded in a room searching for an exit, and no one told you there wasn't one. And on the other side was the best damn party you'd ever heard. You were just at that party, and it was amazing.
You kept looking for the exit. Hands outstretched, holding onto anything in the black space around you. But you'd never find the door. You'd never make the party.
Some people would search forever. They'd fill their room with other people, also blindfolded. There was safety in numbers. And strength in numbers.
Some people -- I didn't know how -- but they'd make a door. They'd bust down the walls to get to that party and live to tell it.
Then there was me. I took my blindfold off a long time ago. I sat in the middle of the room, listened to the party and thought, "Eh." I knew there wasn't a door. I knew I wasn't going to the other side. So I resigned. I was resigned.
This? This coming home and walking away, this was my fuck you. I wanted to throw my own goddamn party.
I didn't know if this apathy was me or the thing. I didn't know how much that mattered. I accepted that we were one. When you sat sobbing in a bathtub, listening to your mother scrub your shit out of your friend's carpet, you learned to accept.

"What is taking them so long?"
I sat cross-legged in a chair across from my mom and cracked my fingers. They were the thinnest they'd ever looked.
My vision came back on the drive over. Little pieces of clarity at a time. Now the fluorescent light was blinding; I blocked it with Mom's brown sunglasses.
I didn't want her there. I hated watching her face when they

clinically explained what was happening. She always hoped the words she didn't understand were positive ones. We'd met with an Omaha oncologist who asked about this morning and, of course, took vials of precious, contaminated blood. Then left us there to think. For far too long.

Though this doctor and I had never met, our patient/specialist dance was well-rehearsed. Old pros. We were impersonal and nuanced, succinct and clear. I answered the questions without emotional attachment, like a report. I stared ahead, thinking of the color silver, the skin between your mouth and nose, the Fraggles. I put my arm out when they asked for it. I winced at the needle in my arm, still. My one concession. I breathed deeply and exhaled. I was a model patient.

They made the obligatory amount of eye contact. They extended the box of tissues to my mother. They stopped short of a date for our next appointment. They were paid well for all of this.

I hummed Elliott Smith. A man who stabbed himself in the heart twice just to have the luxury of death. He made me feel like it wasn't really that bad.

I wondered if I'd meet him. Perhaps I'd be him.

My mom tried to busy herself, to brace herself. She huddled her arms in her sweater. She peeked out the window, wondering what the construction crew was building. She pushed my hair back from my face.

I remembered being five at my pediatrician's appointment with Mom. It was kindergarten round-up time, and I had to get my shots. I had no idea what to expect.

I knew my mom had been emotional all morning. She kept stroking my hair and apologizing. I thought she was sorry I had to go to school. I was ecstatic to go kindergarten. But that wasn't it. It was because she knew I was getting shots, and I didn't.

My pediatrician was enthusiastic. I saw her once a year, so she was a familiar stranger. She had cold hands and a cold stethoscope that she'd warm with her breath. A soothing voice.

She rubbed an antiseptic wipe across my tiny arm. It smelled like alcohol. My mom cringed and wrung her hands. Her nerves alerted my nerves, but I trusted the moment. She bowed her head and started praying. I didn't have enough time to react.

"Okay Jorah, this is gonna pinch, but it'll be -- whoops, all done."

Before I knew it, I was scooped into my mother's arms. She was crying over the top of my head, speaking in tongues. Something about betrayal. There was a cotton ball and a *Fraggle Rock Band-Aid* on my arm, and I had absolutely no idea what had happened. No pain.

It was kind of the same, I guessed.

Mom held it in a little more, for my sake, but never all the way. And I have played willfully, blissfully ignorant. No pain.

I know it sounds silly but it's true.

I had almost convinced *me* that I was fine.

I was still a mobile, laughing, eating, shitting, fucking human being with plans and good looks and --

Somewhere in the back of my mind I was convinced they had gotten it all wrong and I would still have years and time and all the good shit everyone else got.

I thought, probably, denial had been my very best friend.

But I had the notion those days were over. That I had taken a turn I couldn't pretend I hadn't. That I had used my final days for things like panty tossing and corn shucking.

The doctor re-entered the room. My throat went dry as I put on my face. The impenetrable fortress of someone trying not to care. I braced myself for the three words I knew were inevitable.

"Mom, we HAVE to go get ice cream," I asserted in the car, anything to stop her sniffles. Jesus Christ, stop crying already.

"You want ice cream?"

"Don't you?"

"Sure."

She looked over her shoulder and pulled out of the parking lot. I knew just where we were going. The Goodrich we used to go to when I was a kid. Even when I was a teenager.

I swore to god, that was yesterday.

We didn't say anything. I turned up the radio, to enforce our silence.

Pop music was so awful. Rock was dead. Maybe I'd meet Rock. Perhaps I'd be Rock.

If I could have come back as anything, it would have been rock and roll. I'd be grungy as fuck with a badass scream. All edges and heart.

Mom drove with one hand on my knee. I wanted to shake it off, but I didn't. Because, actually, I didn't want to.

I wanted her to hold on to me with everything she had. I wanted her to touch the body she made whenever she needed it. I wanted my knee to always be poking over the seat toward her. I sat cross-legged in cars.

We pulled up to the shop and got out without a word. We took our turn at the counter and ordered. We didn't peruse the flavors. We knew what we wanted.

Peanut Brickle for Kim. Bubble Gum for Jorah. It had been that way our whole lives.

Mom paid. We barely looked at each other. I wanted to look at her, but I couldn't. Because, actually, I didn't want to.

I wanted to know her sunshine face as young as it usually was.

Bright eyes.

Lips full of ice cream. Nothing else.

I also wanted to look at her as much as I could, while I could.

Everything was like that. I didn't have any balance. Everything was all or nothing.

I turned and looked at Mom. All my strength spilled from my body. I slumped into her arms, and she collapsed to the ground beneath me and held me. She just held me there and let me fall apart. And the lies I'd been telling myself fell away.

There was nothing but her heartbeat and my sorrow and this cold, hard floor. I said her name, over and over -- like it was the only word I knew.

At one time, long, long ago -- it was the only word I knew.

"Mommy. Mommy," I said. I said like she could have made it better. She rocked me back and forth. Like her baby.

"I don't want to leave you."

She pulled me tighter because that was all she could do to make it better.

# 26
## The Dream

I was born somewhere in the woods. Someone's backyard.
I cracked out of an egg and already had my legs underneath me. They stretched into the soil. Mud caked on my soles.
I looked up and there was smoke. It peered through the canopy all the way up there, at the top of the world.
I saw my grandmother's face. She was a cloud. Or an apparition. Or also smoke.
I was naked and I was warm. I was thin. I could see my own bones. I was a skeleton.
There were trees all around me. Redwoods. I was somewhere on a coastline.
For a second, I was taller than them, I looked down, and I was short again.
I ran. My knees didn't creak. They bent and propelled. My hair didn't exist. And it flew behind me like a wing.
I pushed in deeper. My feet bled onto the sticks and rocks underneath them.

I would stay there. I was running so fast I was flying. I barely touched the ground, and my feet still bled. Droplets. Red and glistening. But I didn't go back for them.

There was a net up ahead. It would catch me, and I sped up to run through it. If I went fast enough, maybe I'd split into hundreds of square fragments and then back together again.

I pushed in deeper. My tongue wagged out of my mouth like a dog in a hot car with a window that was just his.

The net disappeared, and I was still one.

I laughed and looked up. My grandmother was there and the smoke was darkening. There was only a patch of sky now, where the whole sky used to be.

I winked at her and bled onto the rocks. Trees sizzled, and I knew if I touched them, I'd burn.

So I twisted and turned through them when they were close. My skin singed. It wasn't enough to slow down too much.

There were no flames. Just red heat. They burned from the inside out. One caught me, creating a gash on my arm.

The gash smoked. It sputtered blood like an oil can. I felt nothing. I held my hand to it; I looked down, and there was a fire in the crevices.

I looked back and there was blood on the tree. I pushed deeper and then there was a cliff.

I was on the coast of somewhere because it was all ocean and rock down from me.

I looked up, and my grandmother was gone -- smoke billowed toward what was left of blue sky.

I looked back, and the forest was bleeding and crying.

I looked forward, and my mother was standing over the water with her back turned to me.

I looked down, and I was on fire inside the cuts on my body.

And my body was thin. I could see my bones. I looked back, and the forest was laughing. I looked ahead and my mother was

laughing, holding her belly.
I looked up, and the sky was black.
I looked down, and the ocean was bleeding.
I looked down, and I wasn't there.

# 27
## What Love Is

*Text me a picture of you.*

ALEX.
Mmmm.
I spent the next fifteen minutes angling my body to look both perfect and effortless.

*Stop posing*, he sent next.

I shot one last picture and sent it.

When I stared back at it, I was gaunt. The hollows of my cheeks were scooped out, and my eyes were bigger than they'd ever been. And darker. The gold was turning dirty in them. The circles underneath were pools. But he would like it.

He would find something in it, something I could never see. The light was good, early-morning good. Through-the-slits-of-the-blinds good.

Another-morning good.

*Go get your camera.*

No.
I rolled over and hid my phone underneath the pillow. I thought of the camera, in the case, in the back of the closet, with a card full of pieces from the last year. Collecting dust, like a relic.

*Come on.*

I willed myself not to look at my phone but that was never my strength.
Okay. Maybe today was the day.
I heaved myself out of bed with effort. Hands at my sides, I pushed myself to standing, reluctant, but willing to cave. The closet is separated by a beaded curtain. I pushed past the beads, positive of where I left my camera. The only thing I meticulously unpacked and then hid out of view.
It was on a shelf. At the bottom. Underneath things. I latched my fingers around the strap and pulled it out. It swung, hitting the beads.
I didn't open it for some time, I just sat with it on my lap. Taunting me. Daring me to unzip it.

*I will unzip you.* I thought. But I didn't budge.

You know how it is, when you want something, so you just never work for it? You push it aside to avoid all disappointment. It is easier to live with a loss if you never really cared.

I was there with this. What if I couldn't hold her? What if I didn't remember the buttons.
I couldn't stop shaking.
What if I'd lost my eye?
A camera wasting away on a shelf was used better than what I might have been capable of.

*Take it out, J.*

The phone buzzed. I swore he must have implanted me with a hidden camera. Reading my brain from states away.

I put my hands on top of the case and felt it: it's bumpy fabric. I'd never taken the time to notice before. I found the zipper and peeled it to the left until the top flap lifted open. The camera was lens down in a purple cushion. I reached in and dug her out like a baby. Two hands, kid gloves.

"Hey," I whispered. She felt the same as the last time I held her. Cold and promising. My fingers grazed over the buttons and dials, the ridges and slopes. Bet you didn't know the landscape of a camera was so diverse. It is.

I picked it up.

I set it down.

I picked it up.

I set it down.

I pick --

I picked it up.

I lifted it to my eye and peered through the lens. My right index finger shook and lifted to the top.

I set it down again. I took a long shower.

I should have seen more plays.

I should have worn more blue.

I should have written shit down.

I should have sprung for the larges.

I should have made more coffee dates.

I should have watched less TV.

I should have tried a perm.

No, I shouldn't have. Good on me.

I should have karaoked more.

I should have been more vulnerable.

I was making up for that now.

I shampooed my hair, ignoring the memory of when it was long and taken for granted. I shampooed, grateful it grew back at all.

I wrapped my head in a towel and faced the camera again. She sat on my bed like an expectant lover. One I was going to thoroughly disappoint.

I picked it back up and sat on the bed, wrapped in terrycloth. There was this movie I watched as a kid, where a horse diver in 1920s Atlantic City went blind. She was one of those sideshows back before things like OSHA or HIPAA started regulating everything. She would jump on the back of a horse right before it would take a swan dive into a tiny tank, several stories below. One time, she had a bad jump and came back up, totally blind. Everyone wanted her to stop, but her will was too great. She retrained and started jumping blind. She'd listen to the hooves coming up the ramp, and reach out for the mane as it flew by.

I wasn't blind...right now. There was no huge fall, the camera was way smaller than a horse -- but. I understood that. I knew what to do, where the buttons were. I needed to let go, and let it take me away.

I put it in front of me and turned the screen toward myself. These weren't meant for selfies. I stared at it and clicked.

The cheeks were still scooped. The eyes were still deep. I smiled. Click.

I was grateful for the crow's feet. My teeth were big. They'd always been big.

I shot my bony feet, wrapped together at the ankles. I had bunions that stretched my skin to its thinnest. Like there was barely enough left. God, those feet had gotten me everywhere. They used to be my favorite thing on me. Ugly and bony and all.

I sat back on the bed and curled my knees and the camera up with me. I ran my thumbs over her and thought too hard about what I could do next.

Underneath me, the phone buzzed.

*Are you shooting?*

I was still. Wasn't I?
Was I shooting or was I fucking around?
A gate in my chest opened and allowed me to surrender.
*Yes*. I replied.
Yes. I was shooting.

I remembered that I was still in the world. Something that sounded wild to forget but could be so easy if I spiraled into my thoughts at lonely times.
For now, I was still there. I put on my shoes, a jacket, some jeans, and I trekked out into the neighborhood. Down the front concrete stairs.
Had I ever shot these stairs? This was where I lived.
Click.
This was where everything I would ever know began.
Click.
The three windows on the top floor, those ones were mine. Those were where I stared at the moon from. The wiggly iron rails. The unkempt garden. The cracks in the driveway. The neighbor boy across the street who grew up. The hill it was all sitting on.
The rabbit families that had probably created one hundred generations since I sat among them in the yard. The cardinals that flit by. Red head. Black beak. Eyes.
Click.
Up the street, tucked inside the history of North Omaha. Families. Gardens.
Click.
Old half chain-link fences with ivy growing out of the top. The boy at the top of the hill: I had been in love with, went home with. Would I ever see him again? He used to skateboard. Did he still? We used to drink beer and watch GG Allin documentaries, and I thought he was amazing. His eyes lit up when I came around and surprised him on his doorstep. Pet snake. I watched it eat a rat

once.

Click.

The tower of his house. He said he'd never leave North Omaha. I didn't knock. But I did wonder.

Stop sign painted with graffiti. The loser kind -- a tag, not art.

Click.

Someone thought they owned it. It was funny how we didn't own anything. Especially not public fucking street signs.

Grills on front stoops. Kiddie slides and playhouses, covered in dirt from weather and children. When I was a child here --

That felt like yesterday and a thousand years ago. Felt like someone else's life and name and memory.

Click.

I snapped everything around me, half thinking I'd see myself in the picture. Childhood me, transparent and running, or playing -- laughing, for certain. Without a care in the world.

With no loss. No heartbreak.

Miles and miles of curls flowing behind and around her, filled with stars and rainbows and imagination and goodness. I looked at the screen. Old fence. Playset.

There was no me.

"It's okay," I told myself. I was shooting. I was shooting.

Keep shooting.

"You ARE here. You're in everything."

Click.

Click.

"This place will remember you if you remember it."

Click.

"You are a part of things."

Click.

Everything happened for a reason.

Click.

She was in a better place.

Click.
She never even looked sick.
Click.
Our thoughts and prayers...
Click.
Our sincerest condolences.
Click.
Peace lilies and *Amazing Grace.*
Click.
Shaky pallbearers and a stranger's eulogy.
Click.
Blackness. Lower. Lower. One shovel of dirt. And then another. And then another.

"How did it feel, to be behind the lens again?" Alex was excited for me, he called me soon after I returned home. My head clear from the walk and the rediscovery of my camera. He wanted me to tell him I photographed swans and peonies all day. That I rediscovered my eye. That I followed my rainbow.

"Alex, I need you to help me die."

# 28

## What Love Isn't

Days had gone by since my night with Shep.

I hadn't heard from him, despite my calls and texts. I didn't think about it too much, but maybe I should have said goodbye. Said something.

But if he couldn't find it in him to speak with me after having sex, I guessed I owed him nothing. Maybe the choking was too far for him. Maybe he needed to grow up.

I picked up the phone, poised to call him again. I didn't mind sounding desperate. I'd been many worse things than desperate. The days had been colored with uncertainty. Fatigue was the common thread. Sometimes I slept for sixteen hours straight. Sometimes I felt like walks and sitting outside. Sometimes I was in pain and overly medicated. But my thoughts were still mine. My opinions were still overbearing. I was still there.

I put the phone down and waited out the urge. Instead, I texted Alex a kissy-face emoji and waited to hear back.

Our last conversation ended in tears -- mostly his. Yet again, I was sending comfort. He agreed to my request after much convincing. My mother couldn't do it, and she wouldn't know all the important things to do. The way I would have wanted things. He was the only one.

He told me the request was selfish. I told him the denial of it was. And then he broke -- like a fragile levy, he broke. I swear I tasted his tears through the phone. It was the worst sound.

I didn't cry with him, really. I sat there, with my eyes closed, numb. I waited and then told him I loved him. Then told him to get a piece of paper and write it all down.

He obliged. I let it out. Every wan, mundane, over-the-top idea of my final moments, until I heard him laugh at least three times. He unequivocally turned down some of my last wishes.

Skinny dipping in the ocean. A raging bonfire. Readings from my diaries. Burning things that didn't serve in the next life or in this one. Kisses from him and my mother. A photograph of Josephine. A goodbye that felt like goodnight.

There was no beeping. There was no code. There was no machine. But there, listen, there was the life.

Alex texted back a kissy face, too, and our communication was complete. We'd agreed. Communication was mandatory.

My head drifted back to Shep. With whom communication was obviously optional. Why had I slept with him? I'd rather be talking to him and erase everything that happened, than to have one final fling. With him. I guessed, I slept with him because I wanted to. Because we wanted to.

There was some piece inside of us that was forever seventeen, that was forever connected. We cashed in on that. Even if he regretted it, there was no excuse for silence. What did he think? I was going to be in love with him and demand he did the same? I didn't even know if the parts of me that loved still ticked. Shep wouldn't have been the one, anyway.

I came through town, and everything was ripped apart. I didn't know if that was me, if I was the hurricane, or if I was also a bystander swept away in it. Did I create waves and friction? Was I constantly cleaning up the debris or was that a human thing?
I had to talk to Shepherd. I was not going to let him do that.
Like magic, my phone buzzed. A local Omaha number that I did not recognize. I usually screened those calls, but I didn't. I answered. It was a recording.

"The following is a phone call from Douglas County Jail made by an inmate. Would you like to accept this call from -- Shepherd Hughes?"

Shep's voice sounded as cold as the recording, and I hurriedly pushed "1" to accept.

"Shep!" I yelled, grasping the phone with a mighty fist.

"Calm down, calm down."

"What are you doing? What are you doing in jail? Why haven't you been answering my calls or talking to me? I don't want anything to change between us."

"I don't want that, either."

"So why have you not spoken to me? I've been sending you hilarious memes..."

My voice was hoarse, and it was work to swallow. I calmed myself.

"Well. I'm in jail."

"Since when?"

"Since Tuesday. They caught me..."

"Caught you for what?"

It clicked as soon as I said it.

"Ahh -- oh no. Oh fuck. For the money laundering?"

"Embezzlement."

"Holy shit, Shep. How bad is it?"

My head went numb, imagining Shep in prison for years.

"Bad," he said, downcast.

"How did they find out?"

"I had too many people in the ring. And one of them turned on me."

"That spineless rat."

"I know. So they pulled me into the office with a couple of officers and questioned me."

"Oh my god."

"I couldn't even lie. I couldn't lie my way out of it, they had me."

"Dammit, Shep. Dammit. Well, what do you need? You need me to bail you out?"

"No, I'm here."

"What do you mean?"

"There's no bail. I'm here until my court date."

"You have to stay in the jail?"

"What I did, what I've been doing? It's a felony. They're not taking it lightly. It's even worse that I've been there for so long. They trusted me."

I halted my urge to say, "I told you so." I swallowed it to my toes.

"When is your court date?"

"November 12th."

"No, no, no! You're going to miss --" I stopped and thought about what to say, "Halloween! You *can't* be in there until November, Shep."

"I could miss a lot more that that. I could go to prison. You don't understand the magnitude of stupid shit like this. I didn't."

"We'll get you out. We'll talk to your lawyer," I was making empty promises that felt good and sounded right. I didn't know who that "we" was, but apparently "we" could take on the court system.

"I'm so sorry I went MIA on you this week. I knew this was coming. And I didn't want to tell you about it."

"You can tell me anything."

"I was pissed and ashamed and I didn't want you to -- I just wanted to make you...ughh," he groaned like it hurt him to say it, "I wanted you to be proud of me. I was just about to give this shit up, of course. Of course. Now."

"I'm proud of you," I said, without thinking too much about it.

"No, you're not and there's nothing to be proud of. I just -- I didn't think it would come to this."

"Me, either."

"The night...that was one of the best nights I've ever had."

I squelched the rebel butterflies that were taking wing in my belly.

"Yeah," I coaxed.

"I have no regrets about that. None, whatsoever. It felt so right."

I completely turned to mush.

I was not a musher.

But I was mushing.

"It was a total surprise. It scared me, J."

"It did?"

"I think so. I don't know what this means for us, but I'm open to the possibility."

Whoa. Okay. That sentence took *me* by surprise.

We would have made the worst team ever. The dying girl and the felon. Someone could have written a book about all the "what ifs." But Shep didn't know that. Maybe at that point, he should have. Maybe he deserved to know. The last thing I wanted to do was take his heart to the grave.

"Shep. I don't regret it, either. I'm so confused about all of this. I just feel like everything is crazy right now."

"I know, I know what you're saying. We do have to take everything slowly."

"Snail's pace. Slower than slow. Like stopped."

"You don't think anything could happen between us?"

I paused, for far too long, thinking simultaneous, erroneous

thoughts. No, nothing ever could. But if it could, would it?
Alex.
But it didn't matter. I would never have lived here. But it didn't matter. I would have ruined him. But it didn't matter. Because it truly didn't.

"Shep --" I stuttered, mustering up words that could make sense, "how do I tell you this?"

"I know, I know. It's a battle. And now I'm facing prison time and now you're maybe staying here, maybe not. And the whole choking thing -- takes some getting used to."

"Yeah, all that."

I defied the embarrassment I felt. It was just sex. You liked what you liked.

"What do you think? You think we can do this? See where it goes?" he was nervously chewing his lip, I could tell. He was really asking.

A few days in jail and this had been on his mind.

My own mind turned to maybes. Maybe it would be opposites attracting. Maybe it would be the final, beautiful, brief, hot and heavy affair. The one you never got over. Maybe it was Shep. Maybe I did have feelings the other night.

"You know," I said, trying to sound light. "I never plan anything."

"Yeah, I know," he paused.

"I don't know what this can be...it can be anything we want," I surmised, questioning if the words matched the truth. "Shep, there's something I have to tell you -- in person."

"Dammit," he muttered, "I have to get off the phone."

"Wait! Can I come see you?" I stood and shouted, with the pit of my stomach full.

"I'll find out. I'll call you. I'll call you tomorrow. Jorah, I love you."

And he hung up. "Jorah, I love you"?
These people and their tomorrows.

# 29

## Geoffrey

I had this friend back in Austin.

He was a pharmacist struggling with his moral fiber, versus his career. He was one of the bad ones. The ones that hooked you up if you needed it, because he hated the system so much. Years ago, he kept us in a dangerous supply of Adderall, which we misused in the worst ways.

He grew up on a farm in Kentucky, in one of those small towns with no streetlights, a lot of guns, and no black people. Two Mexican families were moving in, in the early 2000s, and the town held a meeting about it. That's when he knew he wanted out.

"People are educated or not, long before they're told they have to be. You're either curious about the rest of the world, open to it. Or you're not. You can GET curious, but you can't get uncurious, you know?"

We were snorting Adderall throughout that conversation.

"You can have the curiosity beat out of you, worked out of

you, bullied out of you. And a lot of people do. I never did. I still wanted to know what was on the other side that people were so scared of. That they hated so much. What's a Muslim? What's a thug? Why is abortion bad? Why is gay bad? I don't know when I started knowing that was all hogwash --" some Kentucky stayed.

"But I knew they was keeping a big old secret from me. Or, they didn't know it themselves. I had to get out and stay curious. I told myself that from ten years old. Don't let any one person calling you a 'faggot' break you down so you assimilate. Don't let any threat scare you so bad you retreat...I had to hold on to that every day. Education down there is like the devil. My mom cried -- straight cried -- when I told her I got accepted to college. Out of sadness. Who in the hell does that? She asked me what I was gonna learn out there she couldn't teach me here. I don't know, Mom. Everything?" He would stop and laugh at these memories, with his head down, while crushing little orange pills. He reminded me of a mad scientist. Long hair, parted down the middle. Glasses. A laugh that came from a dark place. There were the things he said, which were always followed by the visible thoughts he had held in. Expressive faces.

I said he was my friend, but he was Alex's friend first. They roomed together freshman year. Alex said he was a little scared of him, but he remembered to be kind. Scientists were always the weird kids.

Experiments in the rooms. Making drugs from scratch. Being extremely particular about the temperature setting. They both admitted they didn't get each other; the worlds of art and science in a twenty-by-twenty room sometimes collided.

Once, Geoffrey's father came to visit. Alex told me he came in, looked around, and criticized everything in the room. He said the campus smelled like a bunch of pussies and he expected more from Texas. He said studying medicine was a waste of time because the

Jews owned everything, anyway. Geoffrey looked like a faggot with his hair grown out like that. He told him a black family had tried to move into town, but they'd run them off like the scared niggers they were. He reminded him he wasn't no better than anybody else because he was in a big city college.

He said all that stuff in front of Alex, like Alex wasn't even there. Alex said he'd never realized people could be from places like that. I'd never known any place like that. But they existed, and someone we knew was from there.

"All due respect, sir," Alex spoke up from his corner. "There is a no bullying policy on this campus. I know, there shouldn't even have to be one since most people leave that shit on the playground, but it's there. Also, no hate speech. So, if you want to talk like that...you're gonna have to leave. Per school policy."

Alex said our friend's head was hanging low, but as Alex spoke, it started to lift. He brushed his hair behind his ears and grinned, while his dad looked at Alex and growled.

"Is this your boyfriend?"

Alex looked at Geoffrey and shrugged.

"Yeah, yeah he is, Dad."

After that, Alex was more certain he wasn't going to be blown up while he slept.

"I barely ever saw my dad after that," Geoffrey confirmed. "I didn't go home for holidays, I worked. He never came back to campus. Mom would try to put him on the phone with me, and he wouldn't come. I wouldn't ask. I never felt like I lost anything. I didn't mourn the end of communication with him because we were strangers. How incredible is that? How can you share blood and a house and body type and a life of memories and just not know a person? That's psychology shit. I'm not going down that Green Party path. The facts are, blood is just that. A component that keeps your heart beating and your brain moving. It doesn't mean anything beyond that, except what you make it mean or not mean. Mine, means nothing to me, and it doesn't have to. Everybody has a fucking choice about everything they do. And they don't want you to know that. And most people don't want to know that because just going to a fucking Subway sandwich shop and picking out toppings is too overwhelming, you know?"

We had endless conversations like that. Over the years, I found him more fascinating and fucking strange. He had a resentment lurking under his surface -- for authority, for society, for normalcy. Well past the usual college-level anarchy. He grew bolder, more curious, and more empathic as we aged. Our late-night prescription drug sessions made way for coffee talks around the countertop, maybe some cake or a joint if we were feeling crazy. A few years ago, we didn't see or hear from him anymore. No more visits. No more mind-bending thought challenges.

"Where is he?" I asked Alex, concerned we should contact the authorities, against everything Geoffrey stood for.

"I got a note."

"You did? Is he okay? Is everything okay?"

Alex passed the note to me with a bewildered look.

"When did this come?"

"Just today."

I unfolded the paper and saw his hard handwriting.

*Friends,*
*I'm off to Oregon.*
*To help people die.*
*Thank you for everything.*

# 30

## Touchdown

I had to talk to my mom about the hard stuff. As close as we were, we were never good at that. The sex talks, the period talks, those escaped us as I grew. I relied on Josephine for those things; my mom was skittish of awkward topics. Jose and I, always ready to tackle them.

The past year had catapulted my mother into things well beyond her comfort zone. I had watched her grow up. Her mind expanded with medical jargon and her contagious optimism calcified. It was a tough witness. I knew what I wanted to say would be the hardest conversation yet, and it wasn't coming from a doctor.

I sat her down in her comfy seat, and I sat at her feet, my arms propped on her knees. I did that when I was younger, when I wanted my hair stroked. She stroked my hair. She looked down at me with a sad smile; that killed. I returned her one, working to make it real. I knew she was looking at her baby. Not a grown, tired woman.

"Mom," I started. The easy part.

"Baby."

"I've been thinking about things."

She swallowed hard, she didn't want me thinking.

"Okay."

"I want to take control of this."

There was nothing. She froze in listening.

"I mean..." I churned back up. "I mean..."

There was no way to finish that sentence, my tongue seized up, and I was trapped there. She gave birth to me. How could I --

"I know what you mean, Jorah," she was stone-faced.

"You do?"

"I know..." she pulled from underneath me, stood, and began pacing.

"I can't. I can't let you do that," she shook her head as if that was it. "You don't know what could happen. You could do that and then --" she stopped but her hands kept going. "And then..."

"And then what, Mom?"

Her pacing halted. She looked at me with a helpless toss of her hands.

"I never want to wake up and I am completely powerless again. Do you know what that does to me? As a person, Mom."

I worked to make her meet my gaze.

She did, with painful reluctance.

"As a person, Mom. Look at me. I'm a shadow."

"You're beautiful. You're still so smart, you're active."

"No," I asserted. "Mom, that is fading. That is all going away and what it leaves behind? I don't want to live like that. For weeks maybe. Even for a day. And it is coming, no matter what I look like. We know how this ends."

I was lifted and empowered, by my own unminced words, and their truth. That wasn't permission, it was acceptance.

She stopped. Her face dropped. Her hands relaxed. Her brain went black.

"I want you to fight," she whispered, and I wanted to slap her. All I could muster was laughter. A silent humorous exhale of complete disbelief.

"What? You want ME to fight?"

"That's not --"

"When I've been doing exactly what the past eleven months?" I screamed and felt myself losing whatever control I had left.

"My fat fucking face! Needles and puking and all those nights," I shook, zero to one hundred in a heartbeat. "You were there! What was that if not a fight? What more do you want?"

She broke down, holding her face.

"The only reason you get me like THIS is because I made a choice. I walked away from all that bullshit. You don't remember... what I've gone through?"

"You just look so good. I just thought --"

"Did I look good at Shep's? Covered in my own shit, naked, blind?"

"Of course not."

"So, then. That *is* the future."

I'd leaped to my feet, roving back and forth like a wild animal. I felt wild. I could have sprouted hair and fangs. I stopped and looked at her; I took another bite.

"This isn't a WE thing. This is me. And I am done."

She hid as much of her face as she could behind her hands.

"I'm trying to let go," she eked out. "But I'm trying to hold on."

"I know," I softened. "But you're not getting it. I am never going to shit myself like that again."

She nodded.

"I'm not having needles pushed through my skull again."

She nodded.

"I am never going to be without my faculties again. I, cannot."

She nodded.

"So be with me fully, while you can. Please."

She moved her hands from her face to around my neck and dug down deep. I squeezed her back with my meager strength. So she knew. So she always remembered.

"I respect you," she told me in a clearing she made. The anger subsided, and I could breathe again.

"You remember how I was born?"

"Two weeks late. Of course, I remember."

"You said it was my choice, and there was nothing the doctors could do about it."

"Nowadays they just cut you out."

"Yeah. They do."

I didn't go into the details with Mom, which I'd worked out with Alex. I wrote them down for her and folded them into an envelope. I put it in her hand and held it there, taking in the moment.

"This is what you need to know about it. Just read it when you can. But don't wait too long."

She nodded and slipped the envelope into the pocket of her jacket.

My days had been bipolar.

There were days I could will myself into normalcy, days it came with ease. If the day was flawless, I could forget for a moment my plight. I was just a person in the world, not a patient. On the bad days...well, I'd shared the worst. But there were things I hadn't shared. Things I kept so close to the chest, they could be a missing rib. I'd seen Josephine every day for days. Seen her like she was real again.

She was flesh and blood and human. Not some apparition or figure floating above me. But sitting on the edge of my bed, with her hand on my leg, underneath the blanket. I felt the weight of her hand there. You didn't feel ghosts or dreams.

She said things to me, things that were only for me. Just like they used to be. Our inside jokes. Her one-liners. She shushed me when

I winced with discomfort and petted me when my face became clammy. I felt her cool hands on my skin. You didn't feel the skin of ghosts or dreams.

You didn't hear their voice as clear as a bell, just as you'd always known it. I thought maybe instead, I had dreamed her death. That was the illusion. Of course, she was still there, alive and beating. She was a crazy lady; she would live forever. I must've dreamt the funeral. That's the only part that didn't seem real.

"I want to show you something."

She looked timid, pulling out a familiar piece of paper. Her list.

"I made this last year, right after your diagnosis, actually. The worst day of my life."

There were worse to come.

"You inspired it. All things you've done," she shoved it at me, and I didn't know how to react. "It's a bucket list," she let me know.

I took it from her, seeing the plans on it all over again. She'd crossed out the ones she'd done.

"That's what the diving was all about. Australia," she put her hand to my face, palm on my jawline.

"You have lived more life in your time than I even knew was possible. You never let anyone hold you back or put you in their bubble. Do you know I'm still learning how to do that? Still. So I made this to remind me to be more like you. More like my strong, independent daughter. I can't take away that independence now."

"Mom," I pulled her in so sweet.

She pulled back, wiping her face.

""I've never even seen the ocean," she laughed, wiping her face. "Can you believe that? Never seeing the ocean until you're sixty?"

"I want to do that one. I want to do that one with you."

# 31

## Yellow Roses

My pillow was drenched in sweat.
I stank. I could tell. I pulled myself up in the bed, my back to the headboard, and looked around the room. My vision was clear today.
I took a minute to appreciate that.
My feet tingled, and I dangled them over the bed, shaking them out in hopes they would get me to the bathroom. There were always those little sick trade-offs.
Would you rather have your feet or your eyes? Your tongue or your stomach? Shit was so brutal like that. Your fingers or your breath. It picked and chose for me, all I could do was hope it was in my favor.
Hmm. I was depressed. I was fuzzy. I was alive.
The doorbell rang. I peeked out the window and saw a car I did not recognize. Maybe it was Laith.
Maybe it was the hospital coming to take me away. They couldn't have taken me. They couldn't have forced me out. I wouldn't have

gone. I would have tied myself to the bed. My mom wouldn't have let them take me. She'd have protected me.

I stood up and darted around the room. I knew that I was doing it, but I didn't know why. I knew that it wasn't doctors, but I couldn't tell it that. So we just kept darting around the room.

The body worked fine. Would you rather be sane or move around the room?

I'd move. I'd move. Let's dance.

Mom was behind me, watching. Delighted.

"You seem to be feeling well, babe! Look at you!"

She couldn't see the other side.

She couldn't see the other side.

"Yeah," we said, quick and fast. Knees bent one way and then the other. "Yeah." Fast again.

"So, Stassi is downstairs."

I told my brain to stop. Stop moving. Stop freaking the fuck out. Let emotion step in, please. She obeyed, and I started to laugh. Chuckling behind my teeth, shoulders bouncing. I held my hands out. I didn't know why.

Neither did my mother, as she closed the door and stepped closer to me.

"Jorah, are you okay? You want me to tell her another time?"

"No!" I couldn't stop laughing, I almost doubled over. "No, now's fine Mo-Mo-Moooom."

I laid back down on the bed and tried to calm myself, feeling the beginnings of pee threatening to follow suit and lose control.

I clenched.

"Tell her," I said, trying to force myself down and losing, "tell her I'll be right down."

"Do you need anything?"

"A new temporal lobe," and the hilarity picked up again as she closed the door.

There were so many words for laughter.

Chuckle, giggle, guffaw, howl, crack up, titter, chortle, chuckle, wait, I said that one. Yes, I said that already. So then. What was I talking about? Words. Yes. So many words for something else. Else. Other. Additional. Extra.

I walked down the stairs, clinging tightly to the rail, barefoot so I didn't slip. I heard Stassi's voice and cringed, wanting to run to my sweaty pillow and hide. She was making small talk with my mom. Ire washed over me because she didn't deserve the company of Kim.

But I rose above. I didn't really rise above, I hovered. I came around the corner to where they were.

"Hey."

"Oh, hi," she turned with a jump.

I sighed. Please don't act so surprised to find me here. Let the act begin.

"How are you feeling, J?" Mom asked me, giving me an out.

"I'm okay right now."

"Oh, are you sick? You look sick."

"Don't worry. You can't catch it. Let's go upstairs."

Without a word, Stassi grabbed a bouquet of long-stemmed roses and followed me up the stairs and into my room. There was no small talk to be had. I beelined for the comfortable hole in my bed. Stassi stood away from me.

"I brought you flowers," she lifted them out to me. "I know you hate flowers, but they're yellow roses."

I looked at them. They didn't look yellow.

"They're for friendship," she said awkwardly. "That's what they stand for."

I took them from her and held them. They were pretty. They might have been beautiful. But they didn't look yellow.

"Thanks, Stass," my voice was robotic.

"I won't keep you too long since you're not feeling well. Can we talk?"

"Sure."

Stassi nervously looked around the room, distracting herself with other things.

"This is just like it used to be."

"Yeah, Mom recreated my teenage years."

"Look at these pictures. You and Shep, aww."

She got closer to the pictures, examining them.

"Look at us."

"I know, right?"

"It feels like yesterday. But, it was a lifetime ago," she said.

"Several lifetimes ago."

"I mean, have you changed? I don't know if I've changed."

"I've changed. About a hundred times over. But I'm still the same."

"Yeah," she lowered her eyes with a thoughtful sigh and turned to me. "Is that the blanket I made you?"

"It is."

"Perfect colors for you."

"I think so, too."

I patted the white, brown, green, and blue pieces of blanket. I had asked for something that looked like the earth, and she came up with that, years ago. It still wasn't finished. That seemed right, though. I laid the yellow flowers on top of it. It all looked gray. Stassi sat on the bed across from me. It was that feeling when you knew you were going to have to face some things, and no one wanted to do it. You just hoped it ended well.

I couldn't believe Stassi was here; I couldn't remember a time she'd taken the first step in anything. I would sit in that strange silence until she was ready to say what she had come to say.

"I wanted to say that I'm sorry."

My eyes blinked with disbelief. I marked the date and time and then reminded myself to stay humble.

"I thought -- I have thought a lot about what happened. And I feel awful. The things we said about you," her eyes drifted toward the ceiling and she shook her head. "The fact that you heard them. I mean the whole thing. I'm embarrassed."

"You're apologizing because you're embarrassed?"

"Because you were right, you didn't deserve that," she looked at me.

I searched for signs of sincerity. I supposed if she hadn't meant it, she wouldn't have been there. Trying. That was all you could really ever ask anyone to do.

"I appreciate that," I nodded, questioning how I really felt. That would have been the perfect time to burst into spontaneous laughter.

"Okay good. So, friends? I hate the idea that you're mad at me."

Friends?

Friends. Comrades. Buddies. Pals. Besties. Chums. Cohorts. Allies. You want to be friends?

"Why is your family so fucked up?" I asked, my face contorted in a scowl.

"Excuse me? My family is amazing."

"Yeah yeah yeah yeah yeah yeah yeah yeah --"

"What are you doing?"

"They're fucked up. You're fucked up. You THINK you're so fucking nice and innocent, but you are all two-faced, Nebraska gross ass, fake --" I felt my body standing slowly underneath me, my arms curled into monstrosities, my back hunched like a long vomit. Only it was words I couldn't control.

"Insecure, hypocrite assholes, judgmental cunt-face demons and the rules. Your fucking rules...your rules...your rules...your rules... your rules..." Goddammit! "Your applies-only rules to you!"

We were both shocked and heaving; Stassi pulled a hand to her chest. I was bent over my legs, holding back a wretch.

"What the fuck is wrong with you?" Stassi stood from the bed.

"Stassi, did you ever want to see me win?"

Stassi visibly searched for the words but was overcome.

"I should go."

"You can't even say -- you can't -- don't have anything to say?"

"You're being really weird."

She tried to move me, and I grasped both hands to her shoulders, stopping her.

"Stassi, you gotta tell me something real. Something fucking real. Something that hurts you to say out loud. Please."

"Why?" she backed up.

"Because I want to know that you can! That that exists in you."

Her expression was annoyed and disgusted. Could she not see me? How I was begging.

"I always thought if people met both of us, they would like you better. And I didn't like that."

A bell of truth rang between us.

I fell back, breathing it in like fresh oxygen.

"I wanted you to be less you," she shrugged.

"I'm the least me I've ever been," a weary smile melted to tears.

I was my own. She didn't get to make me less me; I belonged to no one. A rapture of all the instances Stassi *had* tried to make me small came over me. The silencing, the down playing, the condescending tones. My teeth chattered, I ran icy cold.

"You take precious things from me," I choked out. "And then pretend you don't know. Pretend I'm crazy for caring."

"Jorah, you're stuck in the past. We've grown up. You look like you need to get some sleep," she took the bouquet from the bed. "I'll put these in water for you. Why don't you rest, hon?"

A star in my head exploded.

"My-my-my-MY Josephine. You took that. You took her!"

"It's just a name!"

I pushed Stassi back with one shaky arm and grabbed the flowers from her.
I didn't know.
I didn't know what.
My arm swung down on top of her over and over again with all of my energy. The roses falling apart, petals pelting her hard and floating to the ground soft.
I screamed, a wild ape.
A living giant, towering over her.
She kicked at my stomach for me to let up, but there was no let up.
Not until the last petal had been wrenched from its stem.

Kim's arms wrapped around my arms and waist, pulling me back as Stassi raced from the room, a trail of roses behind her.

# 32

## On the Wire

I was still on the search for that elusive tape of Shep as a teen actor. It had become a solid, personal mission of mine. I had to find it and remind him how great he was at it. If I was being honest, it was probably more for myself. Shep had no use for drudging up old memories of a teenage hobby. It was I who wanted to remember it.

But maybe because his adult hobbies had landed him in jail, he would have appreciated the memory of better days. He would remember he was good at more things than just felonies.

I could compartmentalize. I could loathe Stassi and love Shep all in the same idea. I was doing that now. Digging through more boxes in hopes of finding a modicum of our history. I kept Stassi in the past, though I lessened her role. I blurred her face. She was just one of the random people we knew back then that didn't make it out of our past.

I knew what happened, but I didn't remember it exactly. It felt like a hazy, drunken thing that I had only half knowledge of. I remembered shouting until I was breathless. I remembered petals hitting hard and then floating weightless in the air. That was when I noticed they really were yellow.

Mom hadn't questioned me about what happened with Stassi. She'd let me rail that day, after Stassi had gone. Rail until I passed out on my own and ran me a bath when I came to. It was a bad day for words. I should've turned down the meeting, but what was done was done. I didn't think I had said anything I didn't mean, but I could have put the flowers in a vase, instead. I didn't want that to be the final time Stassi and I saw each other. Though where we could go from that was uncertain.

I was half-a-foot deep in a big box of my old VHSs. My personal collection. Nostalgia erupted within me, all the things we recorded to save for later, before Netflix. It was always so crucial to be home on time to push record. Unless you had a timer. Very fancy.

A compilation of music videos that I painstakingly recorded, over maybe two years. The top hits of 1998. Spice Girls. Dave Matthews. Episodes of *Dawson's Creek*. I remembered a night Shep was so mad at his mom. He had to work, and she forgot to tape *Dawson's Creek* for him. A major episode, too. There was no website to watch it later. No backup plan. He just didn't get to see it.

I didn't even know how we got through.

Speaking of modern inconvenience --

The phone rang. The house phone. That was for emergencies and bill collectors only. I grabbed the handset in Mom's room, nervous. We weren't paying for shit.

"H-h-hello," I stammered. I punched myself in the thigh.

"You are receiving a call from an inmate at Douglas County Correctional Facility. Do you want to continue?"

"Yes."

The line clicked twice.

"Hi," he started.

"Oh my god, hi. I was just th-thinking about you. How are you?"

"Sorry I haven't called in a while. I have a lot of legal calls. I'm good though. You?"

"I'm here! Oh, I'm so glad to hear your sound. Your, your voice."

"I'm glad to hear your sound, too. Guess what? I'm getting out."

"You are? I thought you had to wait until...something else."

"My lawyers worked out a deal. I don't know the whole thing. I should be out by next Monday."

"Oh my god, that soon? That's awesome."

"Yeah," he said, in a tone I recognized. "I want to see you when I get out. Like, the second I get out."

I didn't know what to say. My eyes darted, trying to think of anything.

"Yeah?" I mustered.

"Yeah. I've been thinking about everything we talked about last time. Have you?"

My face froze in panic. I'd been kind of busy.

I diverted.

"I'm so glad you're getting out. You don't need to be in there; you're not made for that life."

"No shit. I want to see you."

"All that weird butt stuff. That's not you."

"I haven't done any weird butt stuff," he said that completely deadpan. I could just see his eyes shifting around the room.

"You don't have to lie. I'm not judging you, I know that it's not your choice. I know that."

"No, seriously. I don't do anything like that. No one's touched me," he sounded stone-cold.

"Okay, I'm sorry. I'm sure you'll draw someone's eye before Monday. You're very attractive."

"Could you stop?"

"I want you to have confidence."

"I am confident that I hate you."

Okay, we were at a place I could handle. I cleared my throat and tried to respect his serious tone.

"So, anyway," he continued, irked. "I have to ask you a favor. I was trying to have a serious conversation with you."

"Okay. I'm sorry."

He cleared *his* throat. "My lawyers said the evidence is stacked against me -- you know."

"Well, yeah, because you're guilty as shit."

"Okay, well -- anyway. They said the only thing that can really help me fight that is character witnesses. So I was wondering if you wouldn't mind writing one for me."

"A character witness statement?"

"Yeah, about me."

"About how this is something that you would never do, and you're a good, thirty-something-year-old, white man, who got mixed in with the wrong crowd and was too impressionable?"

"Never mind."

"No! I'm sorry -- I'm sorry. I've had a rough week."

"I'm in fucking jail."

"Okay, maybe you win, today. I don't know."

"I really need this from you."

"Okay. Of course."

"And my lawyers will read it first, so if it's shitty, they won't even use it."

"Oh, no! They have to use mine. Yes, I will make it good. When do you need it?"

"No later than Thursday. They have your number."

"Okay. I can do that."

"Thank you so much. Thank you. This has all just been a nightmare."

"I can't imagine."

"I thought I was -- I never saw this coming. I could kill that fucking kid."

"Hey, hey, hey," I shouted, trying to drown out the sound of Shep's voice, "you probably don't want to say anything like that on a jail line. You know?"

"Oh, yeah. I didn't even think about that."

"See? You didn't know what you were doing. Taking all that money."

I heard a slight smirk on Shep's end of the phone; he was loosening up again. I counted the days and realized by the time he got out, I'd be gone. Long gone.

There was no way I was going to see him in jail. But he didn't know that. He didn't know anything. About embezzlement, about death...

"Shep?"

"Yeah, babe."

Nope.

"Umm," I tried to find all the words. Shit, if he were here maybe I could just find something to hit him with. Get my point across like that.

"Shep, I will write you the best damn character assessment those bitches have ever seen."

"Thanks."

The video was buried at the bottom of that big box. It had the name of the play written on the top, surrounded by hearts and stars. That was it. I wiggled in anticipation, popping it in the VCR. It was meant to be; I could enter it in Shep's defense. They could see what I saw.

The visual was grainy and out of focus. It fixed itself about three minutes in. There was Stassi onstage; I blocked her out. Then there was Shep. I turned the volume up and prepared myself. I

had waited for so long.
I felt the stupid grin on my face start to fade.

"What the hell is this?" I asked myself out loud, watching Shep robotically move across the stage. He stopped, realized he was in the wrong spot, and moved to his actual mark, mid-line.
No. That couldn't be right.
I fast-forwarded the tape. I knew he had a monologue in the show, maybe that's what I was thinking of. There -- I stopped the tape.

Shep was center stage, spotlighted. Okay, that was good; I remembered that. Shep cleared his throat, that must've been in character. As he started speaking, it was as if the sweat were cascading from his forehead and into his mouth. The words were jumbled and unclear. He opened his arms at out-of-place times and once even turned to the side -- where no one stood -- and continued talking. That couldn't be. That wasn't how it was.
I remembered him being great; I remembered him being the Brando of our school.
The monologue ended, and he exited to meager applause. Then I saw me. Curly-haired, teenage Jorah standing in the front row, screaming and clapping for him. I knew that moment. I was crying, sputtering how proud I was of him. The scene changed, and I kept screaming his name.
I was his biggest fan.

What else had I gotten wrong?

# 33

## Gift From Austin

The plan was to fly to Portland tomorrow night and meet Alex. He found Geoffrey there, still living his dream, now turned legal, of assisting deaths for those that wanted them.

I wanted.

It was more involved than I thought. But Geoffrey would do anything for Alex. And his distaste for rules had only grown with age. We would take my mom to the edge of the country and see the cold ocean. I would watch her eyes light up with the larger world before her. I would ceremonially burn things in a fire, something I used to do at equinox. I would say goodbye to the loves of my life. Say everything I'd ever wanted to say.

You mixed a drink of Secobarbital. A barbiturate.

You drank it down.

In one minute you were at peace.

In another ten you were comatose.

And then...well, who knew then? Here you were gone. There...

"Maybe you shouldn't watch this now, maybe you should wait until Kim is home."

"It's fine," I sniffled, straightening up. "I'm fine."

I pulled the computer onto my lap and flipped it open.

"Where do I go?"

"Check your email."

The phone balanced between my head and shoulder while I logged in to my email account. I wasn't curious. I was exhausted and wanted a nap.

"Click --"

"Yeah, yeah I see it. 'For Jorah.'"

"Yup."

Alex returned to silence as I clicked the link. It opened up a video on another website.

"This is public?"

"It's private unless you have the link."

"What is this?"

"Push play."

I obeyed. My name floated above a black screen in simple, white script. A familiar song started, and then I was looking at a video of myself, eight years younger in a bathroom mirror. She looked like me, I remembered that night, but I was removed. That was lifetimes ago. That girl had a joker's smile, an evil glint, a heart on her sleeve, a mouth full of positive, a halo of hope. She was wearing too much makeup, her hair was wild, her eyes were bright and curious.

"I don't need no man to make it happen, I get on being free," she sang to the song in the background, looking at me. She was going to a party that night, a Halloween party. That's why the makeup. The camera shifted to a portrait and it was Becky, her tattoos filling the screen with color.

"What is this?" I asked again. She spoke.

"Jorah is one of those people. Hold up -- no. Jorah is NOT one of those people because there's no one like her. She don't give no fucks. She's real. She's deep. She's funny. And you just know you're going to have a good time and end up in a bathroom at some point with a heart-to-heart. Those bathroom talks is how we became friends. There's something about that girl sitting on a toilet seat that just made the whole world make sense. I know she actually gave a shit about me. About my life. I don't know, man. It's not fair, and it's short. And Jorah was an amazing part of it."

I choked back, hearing myself in the past tense. Watching the strongest woman I knew get emotional over me.

"Is this -- did you..." I didn't know how to ask without using words I didn't want to say.

"Just keep watching."

I sat back as familiar faces told stories about times passed. Stupid things that seemed inconsequential the next day. Pieces of me I'd forgotten, pieces of themselves forced into memory. Their tears came in the middle of sentences, in the clearing of throats, in the blank stares. The stares were what got me most.

Those focused in, dreading stares.

I wondered about the thoughts behind them. Examining what would become of me. Asking when it was their turn. Planning things to feel alive. They snapped back into the present the same way. A slight shaking of the head and a deep breath, they remembered to smile and kept talking. They referred to me in the past tense. As a "was" and then fixed it back, as though it was that easy to bring me back to life. A present-tense verb away.

"Do you like it?"

"It's weird."

"I know."

"Thank you."

"You're welcome."

That night, I dreamt nothing. I went to sleep with the outline of my friends' faces in my mind. The timbre of their trembling voices, almost soothing. Burned into my brain for the rest of my eternity.

There was no Shep.

There was no Stassi.

I couldn't blame them when it was my choice to keep them in the dark. I had kept all those people in the dark. I wondered what they had done when Alex told them about me. I wondered why no one called. Why no one freaked out and ran to my side. I wondered if I would have, for any of them.

That was why I felt alone. No one rushed to my side. I appreciated the sentiments, but then they went to lunch after. They didn't call. They remembered, but they didn't know. That was how I felt bitter. And sorry for myself. If they could have been in my place, even for an hour.

If I could have given it to anyone else and absolved myself of the duty of dying young and tragic, I would have. I absolutely would have. I didn't want the burden. I was tired of the burden.

I did more with my life than most people I knew. They wouldn't even have missed it if it were gone. I wasn't supposed to think like that. I was supposed to be gracious and strong so everyone talked nicely about me. I didn't feel nice. I didn't care what people said. I didn't feel gracious. I felt pissed off and cheated and really, really fucking scared.

I didn't want my mind to die. I didn't want my body to turn cold and hard. To rot. I didn't want to be seen, mouth slack, eyes burrowed in, fingers rigid. Formed together with bits of plastic, people staring over me.

I didn't want to know what happened next. Yes, if I could have given it away to you, I would have in a heartbeat.

# 34

## Stream of Consciousness

I just want to feel recognized.
I want to be seen.
Not on some grand level of winning awards, applauded.
Me.
My thoughts and heart.
My most extreme inner fears and loves.
You spend so long practicing life as it's been taught to you. On this surface-level of communication.
The things you do that make people decide your personality.
The things you hide.
The bitter, ugly parts.
The real opinions.
The things you pull off as jokes, to spare feelings.
How many times have I shrouded myself in all the muck of other people's expectations? How many times have I said "just joking" when I wasn't -- so I wouldn't be an asshole.
Well, maybe I'm an asshole.

Why does that deserve an apology?
All the times I've swerved to avoid what i thought were animals in the in street that turned out to be garbage.
How many times have I lied to spare a feeling?
Stopped to give people money on the street.
Brought them food.
Coordinated surprise parties to make people feel special.
Got them the perfect cake.
Stood up for them behind their back.
The times I cried in private because a friend was going through a hard time, but I didn't want to make it about me.
You know, all the things you do in your many days that you don't promote -- because that's not why you do it.
You do it because of love.
You do it because you want to.
Because you're not an asshole. You're not someone to take lightly.
Some self involved megalomaniac consumed in the sanctity of your own drama.
whatever *they*-the collective people you've left behind, for your own self care and fulfillment of your own life's journey -- thinks of *you* is meaningless. Totally meaningless, empty.
You want the recognition.
The people that hear a song and remember one time you said something small, and it changed their lives. The people that seek with you, who understand that thing you did that one time had purpose.
What seems arbitrary, flamboyant, reckless, emotional to some, is a life lived well into the depths of itself. Unwilling to be a good little eighty years and sit peacefully on it's sofa with it's dinner on a tray and watch all the musicians age.
And how you can pull all those things off at once.
You CAN be David Bowie and Betty Crocker if you want.
You can be wild and free and timid and kind and sunshine and

starlight all at once.

I just want someone to see my sunshine and howl at my starlight.
And put me to bed with a song that I like and climb inside my body and know how wide the beat of my heart is.
How sweeping the composition of my thoughts.
All the reasons I bite into string cheese instead of pulling it.
How I will drop anything to run to a party if there aren't enough guests.
How I will load up a car and drive to my friends side -- 300 miles away -- if their voice tells me to.
I don't want to announce these things.
I want to be recognized.
Is that love?
I am loved, they tell me.
I feel that I am loved.

But the big me.
The me that is blood, and jokes, and memories.
The me that "passed away too young." That is "gone too soon." That is "Fuck Cancer." That is "RIP Jorah" and "I can't believe it." Across an afternoon of Facebook statuses surrounded by scandalous memes, and event invitations, and political gripes.

But there is no one to love these little mes.
The little mes I love.
The little mes that will disappear.
That only survive as I do.
That force me to catalog this: to make sure she still lives somewhere.
How egotistical.
How necessary.

The misconstrued intentions.
The objective ways I view things.
How I still want my enemies to be happy.
The things that make me *know* that I deserve --

I don't deserve anything.
No one is deserving of anything.
I just want things.
I want to be seen, before it's too late.
I want to be known.

I've spent so long telling people lies about me to justify who they already think I am. No one is interested in your personal growth, you know. No one likes people to change for the better, you know.
So you just keep faking it, you know.
You just keep faking it.
You just keep faking it.
You just keep faking it.
You just keep saying the stupid shit: "well you know me."
Because even if it's not true anymore, it almost feels like it is. It feels like they're seeing you -- because they know the old you so well, they hang on to it. So you do too.
They don't change.
So you don't change.
And they feel comfortable.
And you feel stupid.
And fake.
But what are you going to do? Stop the party and tell everyone you've changed.
And you're not interested in their gossip anymore.
And you're above that shit.
And yeah, you actually do want kids. And yeah, you'd be a good mom. And no, you don't shotgun Busch Light for money anymore,

but you're not against teaching someone else how to do it.
No, because they don't fucking care.
So you keep it inside.
You just say they don't need to know.
But the next thing you know, you're dying and no one fucking recognizes you.
And you're lost all over again.
Trying to be the person you are and not, all at once.

How fucking lame.
It's so lame.

If you talk about yourself. You're bragging.
If you don't talk about yourself, you're lost -- unless you can just be strong enough to be strong.

I don't have time --

You don't talk in poetry because you're trying too hard to be "deep."
You don't fall in love because it's going to ruin you.
You don't admit your dreams because "no one ever leaves this town."
You don't tell people how you feel because you're "drama".
You don't cry when you need to because fuck crying.
You don't allow yourself to be scared, so you're angry instead.
You don't dye your hair purple because you'll look like "one of those girls."
You don't live out loud because everyone applauds those who don't rock the boat.
But you rock the boat.
Your natural state of being, of living, IS the boat rocker. You're jumping up and down in a goddamn canoe, screaming to all

the fish, while everyone grips their little life vests and bare down grimacing.

She's making us uncomfortable.
We might get wet in this boat.
I'm seasick.
Is that fun? What's she's doing?
I'd like to stretch my legs too.
I wonder what it feels like to scream at fish.
I would scream at fish -- if the others would.
They're not screaming at the fish.
She's a freak.
Sit down and shut up, freak.
You should feel uncomfortable.
Look at the rest of us.
Throw her overboard, she can't sit with us.
Man, this boat is quiet now.
So. How about this weather.

That's how I've felt my whole life.
Bigger than.
Never better than.
Just wanting more.
Reaching for more.
Different.
Something extraordinary, really.
Did I get it?
Did I even touch it?
Would it have ever been enough?

The apologizing is done.
Is it too late to start again?
To take them all back.
To scream at all the fish underneath the doomed boat?

Can anyone see me?
Is anyone even looking anymore.
If I had stayed silent and calm and Nebraska nice and gossiped behind their backs, would they even know I was here?
What was I to do?
Play cards on Friday nights and never leave my home, frightened of the perils of inclement weather.
If it was too hot -- I'd melt.
Too cold -- be frozen to death.
Found centuries later clutching my pearls and saying, "oh my."
Bless my heart.
Bless my heart.
For it's the only thing that's gotten me through -- it's the only thing that hasn't betrayed me yet.

# 35

## SpiritCycle Part Deux

It was Wednesday, the morning of my flight to meet Alex in Portland. Mom kept her bedroom door closed, music playing. She was supposed to be packing, but I didn't want to think about what was happening on the other side. She'd been in there for hours, like that.

I felt smooth. Less fatigue than the day before, more determination. I took advantage of my mother's solitude and went out to her back porch to smoke pot. In the morning, if I smoked it before I had to take pain pills, the chances of me having to take the pills were smaller. Why that shit wasn't legal, I guessed.

The second I popped a pill, I might have been bedridden and woozy. Without the pill, I could think. I could form words.

Everything outside was covered in a thin layer of wetness; I liked that part of mornings.

I reminded myself I had to write Shep's assessment today. I'd do that, and I'd write him a personal note.

I knew the last time we saw each other was the last time we would; it felt cruel that he didn't know that, too. Parting words would help ease that, I hoped. I took a final slow hit from the joint, put it out on the wet porch and wrapped the rest in my hand. It was hot and welcome.

Mom was in the kitchen. She looked up at me and then back down at what she was doing. No smile, no hi. I kissed her cheek with a side hug and kept going to my room. We had plenty of time to reconcile on the flight and the next morning. I wasn't planning on doing anything until the next night. Or Friday at the latest. Friday was Halloween. That would have been badass. All the costumes I ever wore would have had nothing on an All Hallows' Eve death day.

I sat down with my laptop, and we stared at each other. I thought I would just jump right in.

*Shep is...*

Well, he was in jail. And he was in love with me. Both of which were horrible choices.

*Shepherd Hughes is a man who...*

Who or whom?

*Is a man who is flawed as all men are.*

Okay, nevermind. I closed the laptop. I needed to think about that more. I had to pack and think. What did I need to pack? Two last outfits? I'd never packed lighter. Stassi could rifle through my closet just as she'd always wanted.

Oh. Stassi. Right.

What was I going to do about her? I thought I'd already done it. How did you come back from a bouquet attack?

I hadn't reached out again. I sent no apologies.

As contentious as our relationship had been, I didn't want to leave it there. With that awful memory. Maybe because I didn't want our younger selves to be erased, and maybe because I didn't want to be the final bad guy.

What was there left to say? We said so much at dinner, so much at the house. Everything between us was poisoned for one reason or another. One horrible word, one awful deed piled atop us so heavy that there was no climbing out. We had seen the true face of our friendship, and she was an ugly-ass bitch. But a hug. I wouldn't mind hugging her goodbye. For who we used to be.

I knew Stassi would be at SpiritCycle promptly at 4:25, if she were still on her schedule. If things like naked dinner parties and flower crowns hadn't made her want to never leave her house again.

I got there a few minutes early, with hopes of calming my heartbeat, rapid with anxiety. I asked my cab driver to wait for me while I went in, in case Stassi saw me and immediately yelled for security. I didn't know if they had security as an amenity, but I knew the people there were in much better shape than I.

The door jingled. The smell of bodies at work. A hello from the receptionist.

Stassi was already there; she saw me and her face illuminated. One small butterfly fluttered massive wings.

She was standing with the mom group. A ponytail and a fanny pack. I searched for the tall girls. They were in another corner, stretched out like drinking giraffes.

"Jorah, hi!" my fellow UTer waved at me, flagging me down. She smiled back at Stassi in a friendly way. If I had covered her in Nebraska football body paint, Stassi couldn't have been redder. Seething, her chest heaved underneath her social dilemma. I had to make my intentions clear. I walked to her group.

"Hi, ladies. Hi, Stassi."

The strangers said hi; Stassi did not. Why would I have expected her to? One of her fists clenched. Wouldn't that be the perfect cherry on top? If that bitch punched me right then. I put the thought to the side.

"You came back," Heather said in a caffeinated voice.

"I did." I tried to sound enthused, but come on.

The bell sounded, and everyone started to move into the bike room. I grabbed Stassi's wrist as she rushed past me.

"Stass, I need to talk to you."

"You have some nerve coming back here," she hissed, still walking.

"I know you're mad."

"Are you fucking bipolar? And that's a real question. Do you remember what happened when I tried to fix things with you? You're insane. You need to get your head checked."

That was actually pretty funny.

"Stassi, I'm leaving. I just wanted to see you before I go."

"Bye."

She sped into the room, leaving me standing outside the door. I looked outside, waved my cab off, and followed Stassi in. Her eyes went wide and furious. I was the ex that didn't get a clue. The antagonist in a Lifetime movie. But I got it, because I couldn't stop. I went to the last open bike. It was right behind Stassi; she searched for anywhere else to go, and then the lights went down.

"Stass," I whispered. "I'm sorry about what happened. I wasn't myself that day."

"Well you haven't been yourself in a while, Jorah."

A different instructor entered the room and faced us.

"Shalom and hello," she said like butter. A resonate, peaceful tone my voice had never achieved. The room greeted her back.

"Stass, you have to let me say goodbye.

"Haven't you already? Bye."

The instructor spoke:

"I am Vanessa; I'm here for you today."

She flung her lithe body over the bike. She was one of those women with a makeup-less, easy face. Slight lines around her mouth where smiles had been, healthy hair. She had an energy like a flamingo or African black soap, or hazelnut. Natural. She lit two candles from the bike. She looked out onto us with pursed lips, taking us all in for a long, slow time. The hair on my arms prickled. Could she see me? Through me?

"Stassi, we have to hug goodbye. We have to."

"Leave me alone, weirdo."

Vanessa lifted her arms, eyes closed, and inhaled with intent. We all followed suit. She exhaled with a loud, round sound, and we all did that, too. She pedaled. We pedaled. I was pushing past the weakness I felt in every motion. I was slower than everyone else, but if I closed my eyes, I was flying.

"This is just the beginning," Vanessa promised.

My arms stretched out from the handlebars, straight out at my sides like a T. I tilted my head back. If I had been outside, I would have been bright with sun. I felt a breeze, like I was near the ocean again. I filled my lungs with air fresh-pumped from my heart. If I were dead, I would have been coming alive.

"Let everything around you go."

I pushed hard. I pedaled harder. My mind went static. Jumpy. Like it was stuck on a word again.

Go. Go. Go. Go. Go. Go.

Over and over and over.

"You are here for a reason. Your purpose is divine."

I could feel myself falling over, leaning so far to the right that my shoes unbuckled from their harnesses. I fell hard to the ground. Came crashing down out of the sky. I tried to open my eyes, but it was all black.

I heard Stassi's scream. I felt the tug of helpful hands pulling at me, checking my pulse. There was a pour of lukewarm water over my head. I wanted to tell them I was okay. I wanted to tell them I could hear everything. That I was at peace, it was okay. I could still

hear the ocean and feel the wind -- somewhere in the blackness. I tried to tell them I could stand, but nothing came out.
Everything went silent. No sight. No sound. But still the tugs on my appendages. They fell, limp to the touch. Then my entire body elevated. I floated out of the room, flat on my back. Pulls on my eyelids and pricks in my arms.
Hi, Soul. What was going on with you?

My soul was scared and readied. Like a young soldier facing a first big battle. A battle it stood no chance in. My soul's knees knocked. Its teeth grit as it tried to cling and let go all at once. It wouldn't turn to me. It didn't want to look me in the eyes. I patted its shoulder and comforted it. I told it lies, lies the heart liked. I insulted its intelligence with my wistful notions.
Not one more, *everything will be okay*. Not one more. Or it would have killed itself.
Instead, I stood in silence with it. My hand on it's back. Looking on, where it looked on. Into the wide abyss of knowledge and ignorance. Of knowing everything and retaining nothing. A limbo built of our biggest fears and hopes.
Silence. Quiet.
We saw each other. We were understood. That was all it took.
Bye, Soul. You were never mine to keep.

# 36

## Words to Live By

I woke up a week later in the hospital bed. Propped upright, tubes surrounding me, my mother's hand grasping mine.

Fuck.

It had all caught up to me I supposed.

I blamed my need to fix things. But it didn't matter, there was no blame. I was where I never wanted to be.

Mom cried out my name and yelled for someone. She kissed my head, tears running down my hair. The picture was fuzzy. The sounds were muffled. Waa-waa-waaa. Like I was underwater. The room was too bright to open my eyes, so I squinted. My hands burned and itched. I closed everything and shut down. The sensation around me was too much to take in. That perfectly dull room -- too much.

"Mom," I barely said.

"I'm here, my love," she held my rigid hand to her cheek, "I'm right here."

"Okay."

My throat was achingly dry and arid.

"Water," I asked for, on the edge of an oasis. Mom pulled out a bottle and angled it toward my mouth. I could have gulped the whole thing down, but my jaw scarcely opened. The liquid coursed through my dehydrated body like a waterfall, I felt it hit the pit of my stomach.

"What's going on?" I tried to remember what my last memory was.

"You're waking up."

"I got that. I'm hungry. Why the fuck am I here, Mom?"

"You've been sleeping for days."

"What do you mean sleeping? That's ridiculous --" the slow wake of realization widened my eyes.

"I've been here for days?"

She didn't speak, just nodded.

"What -- what? How many?"

"A week, honey. You were exercising and you fell over and then..."

Exercising. I racked my brain and nothing came up.

"You weren't supposed to push it," she scolded me.

Her face was ashen and covered in signs of grief. Long, drooped bags, lines around her mouth. Gaunt and sunken in. She thought I was dead. She thought the last thing I said to her was the last thing I'd ever say to her.

"What's the last thing I said to you?"

Her eyes filled, her mouth trembled. It was gratitude.

"You told me I bought the wrong pickles," she smiled through trembling lips.

"Sweet ones," I whispered. She nodded.

"Yes, the sweet ones."

I tried to slap my hand to my head, but it was attached to a hose or a tube.

"I love you, Mom."

"Oh, baby. Oh my baby," Mom scooted in as close to me as she could and scooped me in her arms, which seemed longer than ever. Winding expertly through the same tubes that held me back. I could hear her heart pounding through her clothes. "I love you, more than anything."

She pulled back and cradled my head in her hands. She looked at me with stern eyes, a determined face.

"I love you more than anything."

I'd never known a sentence more palpable.

"I don't want to leave you, Mom."

"Never. Never, never, never, never."

She pulled me in again and held me there, to her chest. I was five years old. Tiny in her grasp. I cried. I was two years old, still nursing and learning words. I bumped my head and she held me. I was conceived. Swimming in her safe, warm womb. Doing somersaults and breathing liquid through my embryo gills. Her heart beat my name, and I recognized her voice through all the white noise. I kicked at her from the inside and felt her push back from without.

Would I return there? I wondered. I'd heard so much about returning to where you were before you were born. Maybe I'd return to her eyeballs, or stardust, or just a speck of her, which was always there before. Maybe she'd turn into part of her mother. And maybe my grandmother was part of her mother again and we all went back to woman. Womb. Stardust. Love.

The door opened and I braced myself for another IV drip. I pulled away and sighed. Then it was him.

"Alex?"

I couldn't help but immediately start bawling. The ugly-face kind, with a weak chin and all. I covered my face with my hands, and he rushed to my side. It felt like a waking dream. He hugged me, too -- but that was very different. I knew I was a part of him, but that part ended on our side.

"What are you doing here?"

"Alex has been here this whole time."

"I jumped on the first plane after your mom called me."

"You did."

"I did."

"Were you in Portland? Did you go?"

He nodded. "I was there. I was waiting for you."

Mom interrupted us, not wanting to think about it.

"I'm going to go call Laith, he's been thinking of you." She kissed me one last time and exited. For a second, I couldn't remember who Laith was.

"You're here," I looked at Alex.

"I'm so sorry it wasn't sooner."

"It doesn't feel real," I reached my hand out to him. I felt like an old woman. He felt like a mirage. A long-lost love guiding me to the other side. He took my hand. He was warm. He was very much earth-side.

"It's real."

The things I'd wanted to say to him in the moment vanished. I had nothing to say. My head was black; I was happy to recognize him. He looked into my eyes, paid attention to each one individually. I saw myself reflected back. My true self. He still knew me.

"I can't believe I stayed away from you for so long."

"I told you."

"I'm such a fucking idiot."

"Yes. Do I look like shit?"

"You look like a miracle."

Alex asked with his eyes for permission to photograph me. I granted it. The addiction of self-consciousness disappeared in his lens. I could feel my eyes: they were wide and dark. I could feel my bones, exploded past my skin. I felt like a dinosaur. Skeletal, exposed.

"I don't want to see it."

"Okay."

"I want to go outside."

Alex helped me stand to my feet. Oh -- I hadn't stood up. The blood rushed to my thirsty legs. I was a colt, knock-kneed and wobbly. I held on tight.

"Do I have clothes?"

"Yeah," Alex went to my suitcase.

"Can I wear actual things?"

"You can," Alex pulled leggings out for me, I held on to him while he pulled them on underneath my gown. I was attached to an IV pole and a million cables.

"I'll just carry the sweater. It's fine," I said, too exhausted to figure it out.

We walked down the hall. I thought of the movies where someone was trying to escape the hospital, and they had to get a lab coat and a doctor's badge. And move swiftly, but not run, and be shielded by trench coats...

But no one cared. No one saw me. When they did, they just saw Alex. A beautiful, living man. And his poor -- whatever they made in their minds. Sister...wife...charity case. Whatever they made it. I tried not to get glimpses of my reflection in the thousands of floor-to-ceiling windows that godforsaken place had. But I did. At least, I thought I did. I didn't recognize the person walking alongside Alex, so I turned my attention away and kept tucked into his arm. Huddled away so tiny.

Outside it was cold. Alex took his jacket and wrapped it around my shivering, weak body.

"Is it really this cold?" I asked, teeth chattering.

"It's pretty nippy."

"Nippy," I snorted a laugh.

"Are you sure you want to be out here?"

"I don't even know where I've been for the past week; I want some air."

"You don't know where you were?"

I shook my head like it was some revelation.

"I don't. It feels like I was sleeping."

"It's a big fucking deal. They didn't know that you would wake up. It's been a hard week."

I pressed my lips together, trying to make sense of it.

But I couldn't. I'd missed seven days and it felt like nothing at all. But to them...

A deep cough came over me, lurching me over my ribs. It was uncontrollable. Alex came to my side and held me up. The coughing subsided. I looked up at him, circles under my eyes so dark I could feel them. He smiled, and his eyes twinkled. It was so fucking unfair. Did they always twinkle like that? Did I only see it then?

"You're not supposed to be out here. You're at risk for pneumonia."

"I am? What the fuck?"

"We need to get you in."

"No! No, just one more minute," I leaned my weight on him, everything hurt.

"You've been here?" I asked.

"I have."

"Watching me sleep? You fucking creep."

"I've watched you sleep a lot, yes."

"You know I broke up with Kelvin for that shit."

"I thought about that, yes," he laughed. "I read to you."

"Omg," I rolled my eyes with mock disgust.

"What?"

"How Nicholas Sparks of you. What'd you read?"

"*Mein Kampf.*"

"Great. Now I'm going to hell."

"No. No. Some weird shit I've tried to read to you a million times, and you never let me."

"Oh. Poetry and that weird shit," I said.

"Yeah, that weird shit."

There was a moment that we took, both thinking of all the times before when I'd laughed at his love of verse and told him to find a boyfriend. Or a librarian. Anyone but me, I'd say. So many times.

"No wonder I stayed in that coma..." I tried to joke. But there was nothing light in the air except the wispy vapors from our mouths. Alex's was nearly hidden by his thick beard.

"Yeah. I always loved putting you to sleep."

When we got back to my room, Mom was asleep in a chair. She was snoring lightly, and her mouth was agape.

"She's exhausted," Alex let me know, as I climbed back into bed. My bones were too weak to stand.

"She has not left your side for one second."

"God. Don't tell me this shit, Al. I hate that."

"She loves you."

"Exactly. She shouldn't have to go through this. I wish I'd just been hit by a truck or something. Then it's quick and over with."

"And she never gets to say goodbye. That's cruel."

"Well, it's all fucking cruel. And if I want to get hit by a truck, so fucking be it."

"Okay. So. So be it then," he said it so calmly that I cringed.

"I'm sorry."

"Don't be. It's your party."

He sat on the bed with me, against my legs, rubbing them underneath the sheet. I didn't know what he was thinking. I didn't want to know.

"I feel sick," I told him.

"They said you may after waking up. I'm so happy you woke

up."

"Yeah?"

"You have no idea. I was terrified. I thought I was never, ever going to talk to you again. I can't describe it, J. It was the end."

"I don't even know where I was. I was asleep."

"You said that."

"I did?"

"No white lights and harps?"

"No. Just sleep. Like one of those naps you don't mean to take and you just lose track of yourself? By the time you wake up it's 10 pm anyway."

"Ha. Yes. I know."

"Like that."

"Could you hear me?"

"Maybe? I don't remember."

"Wow."

He scratched his face, eyes steeled and looking ahead.

I loved his profile. Big nose, soft lips, rock jaw. All mine. I swore I still felt like he was all mine. Like I'd claimed ownership of a wild thing, and I was about to leave him to fend for himself all over again. It was not one-sided. As much as I belonged to myself, I belonged to him. I wanted to. I wanted to be solely and only and lovely just his. I wanted him to breathe and eat my name, my heart, my soul. So connected, entwined, that our blood beat both cancer and health, our bodies both dead and alive, our souls both known and unknown. There was no me without Alex.

Well, there was no me at all. Just him. Maybe that was how I planned to be immortal. Consuming the living.

"Alex."

He looked at me, his eyes red with tears yet to fall.

"Would you read me some poetry?"

He smiled so big. White teeth in black hair.

"Yes."

I scooted over so he could climb in next to me, as tight as ever. He put his arm around me and kissed my head. He started with a breath, and I interrupted.

"You don't have your book."

"I don't need it."

"Oh."

He hunkered back in, and I put my head in a cozy corner of his neck.

*How can I keep my soul in me, so that*
*it doesn't touch your soul? How can I raise*
*it high enough, past you, to other things?*
*I would like to shelter it, among remote*
*lost objects, in some dark and silent place*
*that doesn't resonate when your depths resound.*
*Yet everything that touches us, me and you,*
*takes us together like a violin's bow,*
*which draws *one* voice out of two separate strings.*
*Upon what instrument are we two spanned?*
*And what musician holds us in his hand?*
*Oh sweetest song.*

I wept into his arms. My body convulsed in happiness to be with him, in gratitude to feel felt. He was reading my mind again. As one. Alex was weeping, too, holding me so tight I might have broken.

"Did you write that?" I asked, to lift us out of the darkness where we could go.

"No!" he roared with a laugh, wiping his face. "That's Rilke, you asshole."

"Alex," my voice, I hardly recognized. He didn't answer. "I'm ready to get the fuck out of here."

# 37

## TIME

I PACKED THINGS FROM MY ROOM.

One small box, I promised myself. The most important things, I would burn.

The blanket from Stassi. The VHS of Shep. I wanted no one to see that, and I would never bring it up to him again.

Well, I guess I really wouldn't.

When I'd missed the deadline from his lawyers, he had frantically tried to get a hold of me. He found Kim, and she told him the everything. There was nothing he could do, still sitting in his cell, and I didn't call him myself. The full withdrawal was feeling like the right thing to do. Dying didn't have any rules. Maybe that was why I was killing it.

I left the picture of me and Shep for Mom.

I spent the last night writing letters. My handwriting barely recognizable, if I didn't write my name they might not have known it was from me. But how many dying confessions did they get a

week?
Stassi. Shep. Mom. Alex.

There wasn't a lot of reflection going on. My thoughts felt like watercolor. Everything was mechanics and orange peels. Pictures more than words. Touches more than full thoughts. A soundtrack.
I could have laid out songs for everyone that would have more deeply explained how it was for me. But they all meant different things to different people, anyway.

When I moved, it felt like floating. I was alive, a beating heart, inside of a feather, inside of the stone that was my body. Once I cracked the stone, ended it's breath, I would be free.
It was the last step.
Everything I saw was blue. Shades of it, shadows in gold. My mother was lavender. My Alex was earth.
They balanced me there. When I rested, it was deep and for hours. There was no smell of food that excited me. And I didn't want to talk. I wanted my hair stroked. I wanted my arm caressed. I wanted 90s rock on repeat.
I wanted a story.
When I was awake, I was slow. I smiled more than talked, and my sarcasm was trapped inside. Which was torture.
I wrote out "fuck," because it reminded me of who I was.
I could talk, but I didn't have the words to say what it was I was meaning.
I knew that Jorah was there. But I recognized that Jorah was going.

# 38
## Omaha

The snow in Omaha was what made me miss Texas the most. I never missed the snow when I wasn't around it. I was born to thrive in sub-Saharan heat and jungle-deep humidity. But the snow came down. Those big, fluffy flakes that looked like cotton. Our plane was delayed on the tarmac at Eppley. Back at Eppley for the last time. I was doing everything on autopilot. The only way I got through it. I left my room and walked down the hall; I left the house and didn't look back. I got in the car and didn't watch the city as we drove through it. I thought if I realized that I'd never be there again, I wouldn't be able to take it. I'd have a change of heart and forget all the reasons why I chose the path I had chosen.

I was by the window. Then Mom. Then Alex.

The plane was hot, and I pressed my face and hand to the cool glass. There were people on their cell phones and a toddler whimpering. I wondered what awaited all of them in Oregon. Family, no doubt. I couldn't imagine the tourist demand was high in winter in the northwest.

I wondered what awaited me there.
The romantic ideals I had about my beach "homegoing," as my mother called it, were waning, and the reality was settling in. What if she was right? What if what I was doing was premature, and I missed more good days? More small moments with everyone. I had been doing just fine; I felt okay for a lot of days. What if I could have more of that, wouldn't I want it? What if I could have just a little more time?

I thought about the method.
The drink. The potion. When I called it the potion, it made me feel like a princess. I would drink it, and it would save me. Then, in a hundred years I would have been kissed by a scientist, and he would have broken the spell with a cure. And we would have lived happily ever after -- only not, because he wouldn't have been Alex and Alex would have been no more. No one I knew or loved would have.
And it wasn't a potion. It was a drug. There was no coming back.

It went by so fast.
Like I blinked and it was time to say good-bye.
I was rooted and dedicated to my decision. I knew it was the right way for me. I knew that Alex had done a lot to help me. My mother, a lot to understand me, so there was no going back. I had put them through so much, that was my thank you. I wanted Mom to move on with her life with Laith and give herself space to feel joy. I wanted Alex, selfishly. I just wanted Alex.
At that point, I had him. And I reveled in that.
When I landed in Omaha, I had no idea why, more questions than answers, more fantasy than reality. Wraparound porches and sweet tea.

Maybe I found some answers.
Maybe it was in Shep's videotape. Imperfect and remembered wrong and full of love anyway.
In the roses Stassi brought me. Beautiful and brought to a violent end.
Maybe there was no great symbolism to any of it and I, as I'd always done, had tried to make it all bigger, more painful, more rich. Maybe I should have stopped trying to make anything anything. It was complicated enough as it was.

Fifteen years ago, a girl named Jorah got on a plane and looked out the window and had big, big plans.

I put my headphones in and blasted Counting Crows into my ears, like I'd done back then. I guessed it didn't matter if no one on the planet ever knew me the way I longed; I knew myself. I was spread through lyrics and photographs and cities, and no one could take that away. My arms lifted from my body, and I danced to my favorite song in my seat. I couldn't help it. I had to move; it was time to use my body. And no one could tell me no. Mom looked over and laughed at me.
Alex looked over with mischief and unplugged my headset so the music came loud from my phone. The heads turned.
The boat rocked. People recognized the music and danced in their seats, too. They sang out loud with us.
Everyone knew that song -- they sang it out so loud; I wished we had beers.
Our hands entwined, singing over each other and with strangers, who wanted more, too.
We all wanted more. We all wanted to rock the boat.
So we did.

# Acknowledgments:

I once thought that writing a novel was a solitary journey, this experience has opened my eyes. There are many people I want to thank for helping me cross the finish line on this book. First and foremost, I must thank my husband Rob, who has been my greatest support in life. He's given generously his time, talents and expertise -- he's challenged me graciously, pushed me when I needed it and given me the greatest gift of all -- the opportunity to write full time while staying home with our son. That truly is an American dream, and I'm incredibly grateful for it. Next, that son of ours. For simply being the inspiration behind everything I do and my guiding light to follow my dreams. Even when I'm trying to work and he's crawling in my lap, screaming. Motherhood.

My dear friend and literary guardian Jill Anderson, who's spent countless hours of her life reading my work over and over and over again and never making me feel like it was a burden. (Even when it was bad). I truly couldn't have done this without you, J. CCB's forever.

Other people in this village that have shared their time, edited a line, given me a necessary critique, showed up, and dealt with me during this project:

Kyle Gehringer, Madeleine Radcliff-Reilly,

Jen Costello-Scott, Marissa Berry, Rachel Bouckhuyt, Kira Gale, Daneisha Hall ; ), my mother Pamela Berry, and just for kicks, why not? My brother, Jesse. And my unborn child who gave me plenty of time in bed to wrap things up. So many people have been generous of time, heart, and advice and I am incredibly humbled to have you in my life.

Thank you.

Made in the USA
San Bernardino, CA
28 January 2017